HITLER'S
CANARY

HITLER'S CANARY

SANDI TOKSVIG

SQUARE
FISH

ROARING BROOK PRESS • New York

SQUARE
FISH

An Imprint of Macmillan
175 Fifth Avenue
New York, NY 10010
macteenbooks.com

HITLER'S CANARY. Copyright © 2005 by Sandi Toksvig.
All rights reserved. Printed in the United States of America by
R. R. Donnelley & Sons Company, Harrisonburg, Virginia.

Square Fish and the Square Fish logo are trademarks of Macmillan and
are used by Roaring Brook Press under license from Macmillan.

Square Fish books may be purchased for business or promotional use.
For information on bulk purchases, please contact the
Macmillan Corporate and Premium Sales Department at
(800) 221-7945 x5442 or by e-mail at specialmarkets@macmillan.com.

Library of Congress Cataloging-in-Publication Data
Toksvig, Sandi.
Hitler's canary / Sandi Toksvig.
p. cm.
"A Deborah Brodie book."
Summary: Ten-year-old Bamse and his Jewish friend Anton participate in the
Danish Resistance during World War II.
ISBN 978-1-250-07627-4 (paperback) / ISBN 978-1-4299-6931-4 (e-book)
1. Denmark—History—German occupation, 1940-1945—Juvenile fiction.
[1. Denmark—History—German occupation, 1940-1945—Fiction.
2. World War, 1939-1945—Jews—Rescue—Denmark.
3. Jews—History—20th century—Fiction.] I. Title
PZ7.T57347Hit 2007   [Fic]—dc22   2006016607

First published in Great Britain by Doubleday,
an imprint of Random House Children's Books, 2005
Published in the United States by Roaring Brook Press, 2007
First Square Fish Edition: 2015
Book designed by Robin Hoffmann/Brand X Studios
Square Fish logo designed by Filomena Tuosto

1   3   5   7   9   10   8   6   4   2

AR: 5.4 / LEXILE: 810L

For Teddy

HITLER'S
CANARY

The one condition necessary
for the triumph of evil
is that good men
do nothing.

~

Edmund Burke

The day the Germans invaded I was asleep
on Henry V's throne. It was 1940. I was ten and I was
asleep on the throne in the middle of the stage at the
Royal Copenhagen theater. I suppose it made it all
seem even more dramatic. The real King Henry, of
course, had been dead for a long time, but I had seen
my Uncle Max play him so often that I dreamed about
Henry and his great battles. I imagined I was making
wonderful speeches, calling the soldiers to cry "God for
Harry, England, and Saint George!" I knew the words:

> . . . when the blast of war blows in our ears,
> Then imitate the action of the tiger.

I had heard the speech a million times from the
wings of the theater. It was stirring stuff, even for a
small Danish boy.

That night, April 9, there had been a big party on
the stage. All the actors had done little scenes and
everyone had wept when my mother did her piece
from Hamlet where the queen says that poor, mad

1

Ophelia has drowned herself in the river. Even Torvald the comic cried and said Mama could move an onion to weep. Mama had bowed low and still for a moment and there was this tremendous hush. She knew she had everyone in the palm of her hand because she looked at me and winked. Then she stood up and gave the tinkling laugh that got such good reviews in her production of *A Doll's House*. It was as if all the sad bits had been a great joke and everyone felt better immediately. Remembering to laugh when things were bad was what Mama did best.

Father had painted a little congratulations card for everyone, with the red-and-white flags of Denmark spelling out their names. Thomas, who was wardrobe master, had provided fancy dress and there were kings and clowns, cowboys and Indians, courtiers and peasants, ballet dancers and stilt walkers and even two men from the electrics crew dressed as a cow. Thomas had found me a top hat and waistcoat and said I could be "the little ringmaster." I don't know what I must have looked like in the huge hat and my usual baggy gray shorts, which came to my knee, but I thought it was great getting dressed up. The old season was over and everyone needed to relax a little. Soon there would be new plays, with hours of rehearsal and lots of tension and excitement, but for now it was time to have fun.

I loved the theater and everything about it: the dusty smell, the old wooden boards where anything could happen, the excitement, the nerves, the showing off and the fun. From my mother I learned to love it when the place was full and the audience was hushed. My mother was an actress through and through. My father was in the theater too, but he was a designer and painter. From him I learned how wonderful it could be when the stage was empty, waiting for the next great set to be put up—that moment when the theater could become anything from a sailing ship to a Bedouin desert. My father would stand on the stage and show me the drawings of the world he wanted to build.

"Look, Bamse," he would say. "Just imagine where we will take everyone next time." He and I would stand there and create magic with his paints and brushes and imagination.

We lived in a make-believe world and it was hard for me to imagine doing anything else with my life. My mother was not just any actress. She was one of the most famous women in Denmark. She was what the Danish critics called "a leading light." Elegant and beautiful, she was brilliant at Chekhov, at comedy and, of course, at Shakespeare. Mama and Papa had met onstage and I had been hanging around the theater since Mama had first carried me on in a music revue as the brand-new baby of a girl who had got into trouble. Then there was Uncle Max (who was not my real uncle but my godfather). Uncle Max was a wonderful actor and he and Mama had played every famous couple there was in the theater. I sometimes think the audience thought they were married in real life, they were so good together. They could make you cry and laugh at the same moment. Maybe that's why we were so good at it once the war came.

On the night of the big party no one had been talking about politics. There was a war going on in Europe but so far Denmark had been left alone. I don't remember being afraid, even though in those days I was sometimes fearful of other things and slept with a light on. After everyone had done their party pieces we all sang old Danish songs. The Danes love singing and Uncle Max had written some new words especially for that night, making jokes and poking fun at everyone. My big brother, Orlando, who was sixteen, and my fourteen-year-old sister, Masha, had gone home, but I hid out of the way so as not to catch Mama's eye and make her realize how late it was. I had watched the grown-ups laughing and drinking beer. Then Thomas had put me on the throne and made me deliver one of Henry's speeches and everyone had clapped. I had fallen asleep on the throne with the sound still ringing in my ears.

When I awoke in the morning I wasn't sure where I was. The electricians had gone home. Perhaps they had walked through the streets of Copenhagen still dressed as a cow. A drunk cow heading home. Even at a party the backstage people never last as long as the actors. The men had turned out the lights except for the one safety lamp that always burns night and day in every theater in the world. Now the whole stage was lit with a single bulb on a stand in the corner. The music had stopped but I wasn't alone. There were various sleeping bodies about the place, and Kaufmann, who played the piano for the sketches, seemed to have collapsed across the keyboard. None of the slumbering shapes looked like Mother or Father but I wasn't afraid. This was my home.

I rubbed my eyes and then listened. I could hear a faint humming. Like thunder coming closer. No. More like a deep droning. Like the chorus in *Carmen* heading toward the stage for the "Toreador Song," except without the harmony. Suddenly the door to the dressing-room corridor banged open at the back. It was Thomas, who as well as being the wardrobe master was Mama's personal dresser. He looked frail and shaky, which was odd. Thomas was one of life's cheerful people. He was so used to drama on and off stage that I had never seen anything really upset him. He had been in the theater since he was a boy and I think life for him was mostly pretend. Thomas worried about Mama, or about the costumes or about his own hair, but not about anything else. He looked at me and his thin body was shaking.

"Oh Bamse, oh my God, oh my God, they have come, they have come." He choked as he spoke. "They have come."

The humming was getting louder. Now I couldn't just hear it, I could feel it in my chest. Thomas was sobbing and choking. I made him sit on Henry's throne and waited till I felt I could leave him. He was so paralyzed with fear that I didn't know what to do, but I thought I had better find Mama. Mama would make him all right again. I left Thomas sitting on the huge gold chair while all the partygoers still slept all over the stage. He looked like a tiny king with all his court dead around him in the shadows.

I ran to Mother's dressing room to see if she was there. It was empty. Just the usual props and costumes and the smell of greasepaint, which in those days everyone still used for stage makeup. I opened her window and looked out into the street. Below me the small cobbled square was full of people staring up into the sky in disbelief. The usual bright blue spring sky of Copenhagen was crowded with heavy gray planes. I didn't know it then but they were German Junkers Ju-52 transport planes: heavy, snub-nosed things with their wheels almost touching the chimney pots. They were flying in tight formation over the red-tiled rooftops of Denmark's capital city. It was almost like an air show. They were so low I could clearly make out the white circle with the German swastika symbol on their wings. It wasn't something I had seen much before but it had been in the papers and I knew what it was.

The planes were dropping paper. Green paper. Leaflets. Some people in the street were running and I could see cyclists tearing off in all directions. An old man had paused to shake his stick at the sky.

"What is it?" I called out to him.

"This," he cried, pointing at the planes in fury, "is our enemy!"

The green leaflets continued to flutter down. I put my hand out of the window and grabbed one. It was a strange mix of Danish, German, and Norwegian. I remembered thinking how dreadful my teacher at school would have thought it was.

OPROP, said the headline—ATTENTION.

It was addressed to the soldiers and people of Denmark and said that the Germans had come to protect them from the evil plans of the British and the French; that all Danes were to go on with their lives as if everything were normal. I knew I should be afraid but I didn't know yet what of: the Germans? The British? The French? We were theater people. We didn't get involved in these things. It was nothing to do with us.

The dressing-room door opened and Mama stood there in her shimmering royal gown of the night before. She looked perfect. As if nothing had happened at all.

"Mother," I exclaimed, "I think the Germans have come."

"Yes, dear," she replied. "We must change at once."

ACT I, SCENE ONE
TIME: *April 1940*
PLACE: *Copenhagen*

___This is my story.___ It is my story of when the war came to Denmark in 1940. The Second World War. I can't give you the whole picture of what happened; just what I saw and what people told me. There are hundreds of personal stories from that time, but this is not one in which all Germans were bad and all Danes were good. It didn't work that way. There were just some good people and some bad people and it wasn't always easy to tell the difference.

I often think of Thomas sitting on the throne at the moment the Germans invaded. I wish I had remembered to tell Mama. I'm sure it would have pleased her. Mama lived and breathed drama. As far as she was concerned, there was an appropriate part and costume for everything that happened in life. She believed that it was all part of what she called *Livskunt*—the art of living.

Mr. Shakespeare once said that "all the world's a stage," but I think even he would have been amazed at how much Mama believed it to be true. To be honest, Mama's insistence that there was an outfit for every event was not always easy for the family. Parents' evenings at my school, for example, could be a nightmare. If she thought I was doing well, she would arrive dressed in gold silk and sequins to draw attention to herself as the mother of a brilliant boy. If I did badly, she came in rags and old shoes like a poor beggar woman with no money to provide her poor boy with even a pencil. Who could blame her if he wasn't at the top of the class? Sometimes it tried my father's patience.

"For goodness' sake, Marie, you must give the boy some sense of the real world as well. You can't keep pretending everything is a performance. You're his mother. Have you no proper advice for him to help him along his way?"

My mother looked at my father and shook her head in disgust. "Of course I have advice for him, Peter," she replied in a soft, low voice that could nonetheless be heard in Sweden. She put her hand out and held my chin so that I looked straight into her face.

"Bamse, darling, if you are ever asked to do Shakespeare in the theater, then always play a king or a queen—royalty always get a chair and they never carry props."

As far as I remember, it's the only guidance in life that my mother ever gave me, yet I learned so much from her.

If Mama was the life and soul of the party, then my father was the one who paid the piper. He was a small, gentle man. He was handsome but he had, as Mama used to say, "a face fit for a coin." From one side he was perfect, but on the other a great red stain spread from his forehead to his chin. It was as though someone had poured a glass of dark red liquid over that side of his face and it had stained it forever. I never really noticed it. It's only when I look at old photographs that I remember the mark was there at all, but I know Father thought about it. All his adult life he looked at my mother in wonder, amazed that someone so beautiful should have married him.

"The swan and the ugly duckling," he would laugh when they hugged, which they did often.

Papa was a wonderful painter. If my mother could play Ibsen better than anyone in the whole of Scandinavia, he could paint something so real you wanted to reach out and grab it. He did the sets at the theater and for extra money he painted people's portraits and did cartoons for the newspapers. I didn't know it then, but her acting and his brushes were to save our lives. I don't think my parents knew anything about war before it came. I probably didn't know anything about anything.

It was cold that winter—bitter cold—and by the time April came, there was still a thick frost in the air. No one thought anything about the great merchant ships steaming right past the Danish security forces to dock at Langelinie Pier in the heart of Copenhagen. Everyone presumed that the ships brought coal. They always brought coal. We needed coal. Like I said, it was cold. The freighters sailed right into the heart of the city: up past the army headquarters, past Amalienborg, the palace where the king lived. But they did not bring coal. The boats were like a modern Trojan horse—you know, the one with all the Greek soldiers inside. Only, these were full of German troops.

The morning I heard the droning sound Mama sent me out to find Father and bring him home. I ran out of the stage door into the street and banged into a man standing with his back to the door. I slipped and fell and lay across his high black boots. I looked up and he laughed.

"What's the hurry?" he asked in German as he reached for my collar and pulled me to my feet. He was wearing a green uniform I had never seen before. It was a dark olive color but seemed to be covered in coal dust. He flicked a cigarette away and went to join three other soldiers standing nearby. A small crowd of Danes had gathered on the corner, looking at them but not saying anything. It was as if they were watching a play.

"What's happening?" I asked one of them.

"We've been occupied," said a woman. She spat on the ground and then walked away, pushing her bicycle.

All across the city, people were going about their business but the atmosphere was strange. It was quiet, as if the play had not yet begun. I headed toward the newspaper offices of *Berlingske Tiden* on Pilestræde, where I thought I might find my father. Over at the British embassy several trucks full of German soldiers had arrived. They were herding out diplomats and office staff. Once again several Danes stood watching in silence on the other side of the street.

Suddenly a young man about my brother's age called out, "Hurrah for Britain!" and the other Danes nodded in silent agreement.

"Anyone attempting to interfere will be shot!" barked a German soldier in broken Danish to the gathering.

"Hurrah for the Britons!" replied the crowd.

I didn't know why we should cheer the British. I didn't know anything.

I found my father sitting at his drawing board, puffing on his pipe while he finished a drawing. I had seen him there a hundred times, with his jam jars full of pencils and the slight smell of India ink and pipe tobacco that always lingered on his jacket. I was so relieved to find him. Nothing had really happened yet but I could feel the fear in the air and I needed his calm to make everything all right.

"Papa, the Germans have come. Papa!"

My father carried on drawing. Despite my anxiety I couldn't help but stop and watch my father's pen as an elephant appeared on the blank piece of paper.

"The elephant, Bamse," he told me, "is the symbol of the highest order of nobility achievable in Denmark." He matched his words to the careful, slow strokes of his pen. Papa never said anything unless he had a point to make. He said Mother had enough chatter for both of them.

"The Order of the Elephant is given by the king to only a very few. Curious, isn't it, as we Danes have no elephants? It is named for the great battle elephants in the Crusades. Strong but silent they marched." Then he drew a horse beside the large creature and carefully wrote: "No horse, not even a Trojan one, can match an elephant."

I didn't know what it meant. Papa put down his pen and looked at his drawing. "It is done," he said.

"Mama wants you to come home."

"Of course, my boy, and that is where everyone should be."

My father pedalled his old black bicycle through the streets while I perched on the luggage carrier on the back, my legs swinging clear of the turning spokes. We headed north to our flat in the small suburb of Charlottenlund. Along the way we could see German soldiers in olive-green uniforms with shiny weapons marching across Langelinie Bridge, down toward Østerport Station on their way to Nyboder School on Øster Voldgade.

"They say the school has been taken over as a German barracks," called my father over his shoulder.

It was the only good news I had heard all day. Nyboder wasn't my school but perhaps, I thought, the

Germans had taken over others as well and I wouldn't have to go to lessons. As they marched the soldiers sang *"Wir Fahren Gegen Engeland"* and *"Die Fahne Hoch."* Above our heads black Stuka planes howled, but there was no fighting that I could see. The invaders were marching where they liked and taking what they liked. Suddenly I felt angry. Why should they come here and march through our city? Even though I didn't really know what was happening, I could feel how upset everyone was and I was angry. I stuck out my tongue at a passing brigade and blew a raspberry. My father jerked his bicycle to a halt and turned on me.

"Don't you ever do that!" he said sharply but in a low voice so that the soldiers wouldn't hear. I was frightened. I had never seen him angry with anyone. "Do you want to get killed? That is not how we will deal with this. We will be calm and we will wait to see what happens."

"I don't want to be a coward," I declared, matching Papa in anger.

He took a deep breath and hugged me to his chest. "Bamse, my boy, you are not a coward but you have to think about the situation we are in. I need you to be sensible. What can a tiny nation like ours do against a mighty nation like Germany? We have but four and a half million people. There are seventy-five million Germans and they have one of the strongest armies in the world. If he chose to, the German leader, Hitler, could simply bomb us into submission. No. You must pick your fights carefully and this one is too big. We shall be calm and go home."

We rode out past the square of the king's palace at Amalienborg. People said there had been a few shots at the palace but within two hours the Danish government had given in.

"Is the king in there making plans?" I asked Papa.

"I hope so," replied my father as he pedalled us home. I tried to imagine King Christian somewhere behind the curtains, making a daring plan. I hoped he was, because I knew my Danish history from school: for the first time in nine hundred years my homeland of Denmark was not free and independent.

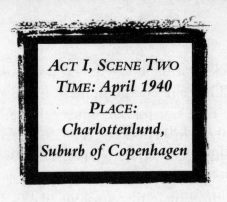

<u>*You might have thought*</u> that the day the Germans invaded would have been quite a big day in history, that the whole family sat around discussing Europe, but when we got home, Mama was trying on hats from Sallie Besiakov's shop in Amager. My mother always used Sallie for her hats, and Thomas was helping her. He seemed to have calmed down since his outburst in the theater. In fact, it was as if he hadn't a care in the world except trying to get feathers to sit at the right angle.

"Now this one, Marie," he declared as he unpacked something pink with flowers on, "this one is so very you."

He and Mama clapped their hands with delight. It was too much for my older brother Orlando. Orlando was not thinking about hats. He practically ran to us as we came through the front door.

"Papa, any news?"

Papa shook his head. "Just what I guess you already know. They came in coal boats. They say the German ship *Hansestadt Danzig*, which is down at the harbor, brought a whole battalion."

"I heard that the whole air force is gone. The planes were at Vaerloese airfield and the Germans destroyed them all in just a few minutes. What shall we do?" moaned Orlando.

"I don't know, son. Nothing for the moment." Papa sighed and took his pipe out of his jacket pocket. It was the only sign of tension in the house. Papa wasn't allowed to smoke inside but he chewed the stem of his pipe when he had something on his mind.

"Shouldn't we get a gun?" demanded my brother.

"No," replied Papa rather sharply. "The government and the king are still in place. For the moment, we wait. It won't help anyone, Orlando, if we just go off the deep end."

"Oh, let's try the green one, Thomas!" declared Mama, paying no attention to the conversation.

Orlando was furious. "Mother, this is not the time to be frivolous."

"Don't be silly, Orlando. This is precisely the time," replied Mama, looking in the mirror. She was wearing a smart tunic and black trousers. She looked like the tin soldier in the Hans Christian Andersen story. Maybe she had decided it would be her military outfit for the war.

"Marie—" began Papa.

"I don't think green is right for a war," interrupted Thomas. "We need something less military. More cheerful. Oh, red—red is always good."

We all watched while Thomas fussed and helped change the angle of Mother's hat. We had seen him do it a million times. Thomas was Mother's greatest professional support, but he seemed to do quite a lot of it at home as well. He was a slight man who always dressed in brilliant colors, like a butterfly with only one day to live but making the most of it. Sometimes when Papa's brother, our Uncle Johann, had been drinking, he would say that Thomas seemed more like Mama's sister than a friend. Papa's teeth ground down on the stem of his pipe.

Orlando looked desperately to our father, who shrugged and went to see about dinner. Our housekeeper was not the best and sometimes she seemed to forget that we hadn't eaten. I didn't know what to do, so I sat down on the floor and began to lay out my toy soldiers.

"Mother, you don't seem to understand, we have been invaded," Orlando tried again.

"And what do you want me to do about it, Orlando?" she muttered as she tried different poses in a large cerise picture hat.

"We should all stick to doing what we do well," lisped Thomas.

"Oh, what do you know, you silly man!" yelled Orlando, who at sixteen seemed to me so nearly a man. "All you know about is theater and powder and paint. That's not what we need. We need real men now, not some ninny with—"

Mama rose up to her full height and threw the hat to one side. She was a tall, elegant woman and could get the attention of an entire theater with the flick of an eye. Now she thrust back her head. In her military togs she looked as if she was about to charge us.

"Orlando, don't you dare," she boomed. "In this house we respect and cherish differences. Let me tell you that the very atrocities you are worrying about occur when people are obsessed by their differences, and that will not be happening in my home."

"He ought to be a man," dared Orlando against this onslaught.

"What ought a man to be? What ought a man to be?" Mother repeated, building herself up to a crescendo. "Well, my short answer is: himself."

It was the second time in one day I had seen one of my parents angry.

Mama sat down and took a deep breath. Thomas clapped his hands silently and mouthed, "Brilliant." He picked up another hat. "*Peer Gynt*, wasn't it?" he asked, as if they hadn't even been interrupted in their work.

Mama nodded. She was always quoting from different plays she had been in. You could never tell if she was saying something she had thought of herself or whether it was Mr. Ibsen or whoever. Whatever it was, she made it sound good.

Thomas clapped his hands. "I've got one—I've got one: 'When the first baby laughed for the first time, the laugh broke into a thousand pieces and they all went skipping about, and that was the beginning of fairies.'"

"*Peter Pan!*" screamed Mama, and the serious conversation was over as she and Thomas drifted off into a series of anecdotes about high wires and green stockings. "Do you remember that dreadful production where . . . ?"

It was too much for Orlando. He stormed out of the flat, nearly knocking over my sister, Masha as she came in. Normally both Papa and Mama would have wanted to know where she had been. She looked flushed and hot, as if she had been running, but no one said a word. Nothing seemed normal and I felt afraid.

That evening my father sat chewing on his pipe while I sat on the floor, laying my armies out in front of the fire.

"You know," said Papa as if he had just thought of it, "Sallie Besiakov—Mama's hat maker—her grandfather came to Denmark in nineteen hundred and five. Came all the way from Russia."

"Why?" asked my big sister, Masha. She was fourteen and she had seen too many Russian plays not to think it rather a romantic place to live.

"He was Jewish and the Russians had something called a pogrom. They decided they didn't like the Jews and so they would kill them all."

"Why?" I asked.

Papa took his pipe from his mouth and looked at it for a moment. "People are strange. When things are going wrong for them, they like to have someone to blame. At that time the Russians decided to pick on the Jews. As indeed Mr. Hitler has decided now."

"So why didn't they kill the grandfather?" I asked.

"Well, he was a hat maker like Sallie. A fine hat maker. He made fur hats for the Cossack soldiers to keep them warm in the bitter Russian winter. The hats were so fine that when the time came to kill the Jews, they let Sallie's grandfather go and he came to Denmark."

"Why Denmark?" inquired Masha, who still couldn't get over anyone leaving Russia.

"Oh well, I think he wanted to go to America but he ran out of money. Anyway, the point is—do whatever you do well. You never know—it might just save your life." He turned back to his newspaper. "Let's not forget the Church of Our Saviour and how badly that turned out."

Papa did that—started a story and pretended he wasn't going to finish it.

I smiled. "What happened to the church, Papa?"

"Ah well." Papa put down his paper and settled back with his pipe. "They say the man who designed it, Laurids de Thurah, made a horrible mistake. The church has a great spire and when it was finished, the king came to see it. Instead of being impressed, the king tutted, 'This is no good,' he said, 'the spire winds to the right. I wanted it to go the other way.'

"They say Mr. de Thurah was so depressed that he climbed to the top of the spire and leaped to his death."

I thought about it for a moment. "I think the king sounds ungrateful."

"Perhaps." Papa chewed on his pipe. "Or perhaps the artist knew that his work wasn't perfect and he couldn't live with that."

Late that night Mama got word that Uncle Max had left on the boat for America to try his luck at movies. I think she knew then that nothing was ever going to be the same again. She went to bed with her heart in little pieces.

There is a Danish word that I can't really translate for you. It's *hyggelig*. It means to be cheerful, comfortable, and cosy all at the same time, and before the war that's what we were. We were hyggelig. Then the giant from the south goose-stepped across our cobbled streets and tried to turn us into pet canaries. That first evening, my father's friends gathered in the flat. Mama lit candles and poured wine. I listened from the hall.

"What's the death toll?" someone asked.

"Don't know about the Germans," answered another. "They say thirteen Danish soldiers dead and twenty-three wounded. No one in the navy and only one Danish fighter plane destroyed in action. The rest were bombed on the ground."

I could hear everyone sighing.

"We didn't stand a chance."

I went to my room and carefully put my toy soldiers away in a box. They seemed pointless and childish now.

My family name is Skovlund. There were five of us. My parents, Peter and Marie, my older brother and sister, Orlando and Masha, who had been born during productions of *Twelfth Night* and *The Three Sisters*, and me, Bamse. Mama had been so sure I was a girl that she had thought of only Rosalind for a name, so when I popped out as a boy, she named me after the first gift that arrived. Thomas brought a teddy bear he had made to the flat where I was born. *Bamse*—it means "teddy" or "teddy bear" in Danish. Papa always said it was a good thing Thomas hadn't brought roses.

In the spring of 1940, we were living in a large block of flats on Trunnevangen in the suburb of Charlottenlund. We lived on the ground floor because Mama didn't do stairs if she didn't have to. It was large for a city flat, with three interconnecting living rooms, which had double doors. Mama used to open them up for parties. At the back of the flat was a small conservatory with lovely stained-glass windows. It was full of dark green plants. My mother loved anything to do with nature and the plants grew wild over every window ledge in the apartment, so it always seemed rather dark and disconnected from the outside world. It was like living inside an aquarium.

I suppose it was a typical home of the time. There was a lot of lace everywhere, and embroidered cushions sent by various aunts who lived in the country. All the furniture was dark and covered in bottle-green velvet, and the walls were lined with framed posters from Mama's productions. One or two of Father's paintings were also displayed, but it was my mother's career that dominated the rooms and our lives.

We didn't have a garden, really—just a sort of yard at the back, although usually you couldn't play in it because of Mrs. Jensen's cow, Bess. Mrs. Jensen lived next door and even though she lived in the city center, she kept a cow. She had come up from the country to marry and had arrived with Bess. Mr. Jensen didn't last long but Bess was a game old girl and went on for years. Bess had no idea she was supposed to stay next door and often used to wander into our yard. Neither Mama nor Papa were cow-moving sort of people, so the great lump used to stay there staring through our kitchen window. Once a year Mrs. J. would have a bull brought in from the country to visit Bess and then Mama would make us go out for the evening. A little while later there would be a calf, and Mama and Mrs. J. would weep and talk about how clever and beautiful Bess was. I couldn't see it myself.

Bess was a slightly nervous creature and I don't think that was just from living in the city. I suspect she had never really recovered from Anton landing on her from a great height. My best friend, Anton Beilin, lived in the flat above us. He was nearly eleven but tiny, with dark hair and very dark eyes. Mama said there was mischief in those eyes and certainly, apart from Orlando, he was the most daring person I knew. If anyone had a dare for Anton, then he would always do it.

Anton and I spent as much time as we could going to the pictures to watch cowboy-and-Indian films. One Saturday morning we had been to see John Wayne, and Anton came back with all guns blazing.

"Stick 'em up, pardner," he kept saying in a fake American accent while he used his fingers as a gun. We were in Anton's flat pretending to shoot each other when I managed to corner him on the small balcony outside the living room.

"Now you can't escape!" I cried, holding both hands out as six-shooters.

Anton grinned at me. "Oh yes I can, pardner. What you don't know is that I have my trusty horse below this balcony. I shall leap upon him and ride to freedom."

With those words Anton suddenly jumped from the balcony. My heart stopped. I felt sure he was going to kill himself—I couldn't think what I would tell his mother but I knew she would be cross. I looked over the edge of the balcony just in time to see Anton land smack bang on the back of Mrs. Jensen's cow. He landed rather well and managed to grab the rope around the poor cow's neck and pretend to ride off. I think he might have got away with it if he hadn't decided to yell "Yee ha!" at the same time. Bess was so startled that she banged backward into Mama's roses, got a great thorn in her backside, and surged forward into the holly bush. At this point Anton lost his grip and slid sideways into the ornamental fish pond. He came out soaking wet and we both laughed so much we couldn't speak. Mrs. Jensen was furious, and I don't think Bess gave milk for some time.

While my family had been trying on hats the night of the German occupation, Anton's had been crying. I found him on the stairs the morning after the invasion. He was sitting in the dark, holding his knees right up under his chin. Under his untidy dark hair, his face looked pale as a ghost's.

"What are you doing?" I asked, thinking maybe it was some new game.

"Father says I should wait here while he tries to calm Mother down. She's gone quite mad."

"Why?"

Anton looked at me as if I were stupid. "Because of the Germans. When she heard yesterday she was hanging out the laundry in the yard and she fainted right into the basket."

I had never seen my bold friend look quite so scared. I sat down next to him and tried to think of something to say.

"Papa says the king and the government are still here and if we keep our heads down—" I began.

"Yes," said Anton, "but you're not Jewish and I am."

I looked at him. I had never even thought about Anton being Jewish. I mean, I knew that Anton and his dad wore a little black hat on the back of their heads all the time, but Anton usually had his school cap on so you couldn't see it. The only time it came up was on Friday nights, when Anton had to go home for supper early.

"But your mom is Danish. She comes from Gentofte. That's only down the road," I protested.

"It doesn't matter," said Anton. "She's still Jewish. The Germans hate the Jews and now they are here."

Suddenly I realized that we knew quite a lot of Jewish people. There was Leo Goldberger, who lived across the way. He was cantor at the main synagogue on Krystal Street in the city. His family had emigrated from Czechoslovakia to escape the Nazis. Sallie, the hat maker, and Thomas and Mr. Kaufmann at the theater and others. I had never thought about it. The only time we went to church was the Sunday before Mama had a big opening night, when we were all supposed to pray for her to do well and remember her lines.

"Are there many Jewish Danes?" I asked my father that evening.

"There are large Danes, small Danes, lazy Danes, hardworking Danes, even Great Danes"—Papa smiled at his own joke—"but we are all Danish. That's all. Just Danes."

It didn't take long after that day in April for everything to settle down pretty much as normal. Anton's mother wouldn't leave the flats, but he and I still cycled about as usual. I think Anton was more scared for his mother than for himself. He was, after all, the most daring boy I knew. We got used to seeing the Germans around, and Anton and I could spot the different ranks by their uniforms. The ordinary German soldiers, the Wehrmacht, wore brownish green uniforms while the Gestapo had black coats and hats and the SS officers wore black with a skull-and-cross-bones insignia. In the harbor, German hydroplanes, which we called Donald Ducks, flew and floated and made a deep, ugly sound. Much to our disgust, all the kids still went to school. Anton and I discussed this.

"You would think," he said, "that being invaded would at least give you a bit of time off."

Whatever we thought, school carried on. Services at churches and the synagogue continued. Jewish schools and kindergartens functioned. There were rumors about things going on in the rest of Europe but this was Denmark. It would not happen to us. People who claimed to have heard of dreadful things being done to Jews were accused of causing panic. We were told to stay calm. To keep our heads down. To be good Danes. My brother kept saying that a good Dane would fight, but Papa would have none of it. He told us to just say, "*Nicht verstehen*" —I don't understand— if any of the soldiers spoke to us and to go on our way. "*Nicht verstehen.*" I don't understand. It was true. I did not understand.

Not everyone just carried on exactly as before. A lot of Danish people gave the Germans something that we called *den kolde skulder*—"the cold shoulder." It's the sort of thing you do on the playground to someone who is being unkind. You just ignore them and don't play with them. Once Anton and I were in the baker's and two German soldiers came in to buy cakes. We were trying to decide whether to buy one pastry or two bread rolls when two men in the brownish green Wehrmacht uniforms approached the shop.

"Yes," Anton was saying, "but if we buy one pastry between us then we still have enough money to—"

The bell tinkled on the door and the sound of heavy boots echoed in the shop. Everything went quiet. It was like one of those Westerns where the bad guy opens the saloon doors and the piano stops playing. There were three or four other people in the shop, waiting to be served, and for a moment everyone looked at each other. Anton fiddled with his cap to cover the back of his head and sidled toward the door. Without a word everyone followed him. All the customers silently left the baker's and went and stood outside. Not a word was said. The Danes just refused to stand in the same shop as the German soldiers. The men came out with their bread and everyone quietly went back in to do their shopping. I thought it was funny, but when I turned to Anton, he had gone. He was running toward home and I didn't see him for the rest of the day.

Another time Mama and I were on the streetcar when a soldier got on and slid the door open to the seating compartment. Almost as if it were planned, all the Danes, including us, got up and went to stand like sardines on the standing platform at the end.

I'd like to tell you that everyone behaved the same; that all the Danes were quietly furious, but of course not everyone agrees on everything. Some people were friendly with our new occupiers, even greeting them in the street and applauding the German military bands that sometimes played in open-air concerts.

Summer came, school finished, and Anton and I busied ourselves with all the things we usually did. We would cycle the few minutes to Charlottenlund Strandpark, with its soft sandy beach and wide-open grass spaces where Anton and I could play in the light breezes off the Øresund Sound. Sometimes we went fishing and sometimes we swam, imagining we had the strength to get to Sweden, which lay just a few kilometers across the water. Other times we went out to Charlottenlund Castle, where the king himself had been born. We would take turns pretending to be the king and his brother Carl, who became King of Norway. We would imagine we were royal and could order people about with guns and soldiers. One day Anton stopped and said, "It's not true though."

"What?" I asked.

"That the king can do anything he wants. He can't do anything now."

We saw His Majesty sometimes: he went riding alone through the city streets on his horse. Christian X was as old as a grandfather but he sat up straight on his horse in a crisp uniform with a double row of shining buttons and a military hat with gold braid. He rode the same route every day at the same time. The king ignored the Germans—he gave them the cold shoulder—but he greeted all the Danes, stopping to shake hands with men who tipped their hats and bowed. Papa used to make a point of being on a street corner to greet him. He said the king was doing what he had asked the rest of us to do. He was showing "an absolute correct and dignified behavior," but Anton and I didn't think it was enough.

Soon the story went around that a German soldier had asked a passerby, "Who guards the king?"

To which the man had replied, "We all do."

I was only a kid when I heard that but I knew it meant me too.

Papa went off to work at the paper every day, and Mama's new season opened as usual. It was odd. Nothing changed and yet everything did. First Anton began to show fear, and then my brother, Orlando, suddenly grew up. After school and at weekends he had been working as a delivery boy for Emil Hansen, who had a small grocery shop on a corner of Jægersborg Allé. When summer came Orlando delivered for Mr. Hansen full-time. For his work he had a large black bicycle with a small wheel at the front, holding a carrier for beer crates and delivery boxes. Sometimes he would let me ride on top of a box he was taking out toward the beach. I remember once we were having a lovely ride. The sky was blue and for the moment I had forgotten about the war and all the troubles. Orlando was taking a crate of Carlsberg beer out to a villa by the beach and I sat on the green box with its elephant crest. Suddenly a soldier, a German soldier, jumped out in front of the bike and shouted, "Halt!" Orlando stopped the bike and looked at the young man. He couldn't have been much older than my brother. They were the same height, both blond and blue-eyed. The only difference was that one of them had a gun.

"Was ist das?" What is that? demanded the German, pointing to the delivery box.

"It's weapons," replied Orlando in German. I think I must have made a noise as I drew a quick breath. What was Orlando thinking? The soldier looked at us both and hesitated. I guess he didn't want to be made a fool of. He gripped his gun tightly and I could see that he had bitten his nails, just like Mama always told Orlando not to do. The German clenched his jaw and tried to decide what to do. Orlando looked him in the eye and the teenage soldier stared back. I was terrified. I couldn't think of why Orlando had told such a terrible lie. I thought maybe I should move to show the German that it was only beer I was sitting on. Maybe we could give him some beer. Everyone liked beer and— But when I shifted on the crate Orlando put his hand on my shoulder and pushed me down. You would have thought he was the one with the gun the way he just stood there and carried on staring at the soldier. Now the Wehrmacht fellow was looking nervous, swallowing rather hard and shifting his feet on the ground. He looked over his shoulder. Maybe there were more troops nearby. Maybe we would be taken in one of the big gray-green trucks that took people who never came back. It felt like we were there for hours.

At last the German soldier had had enough. He gave a little laugh, as if he knew it was all a joke, turned, and walked off without checking what we had on the bike.

"Orlando," I hissed as he pedaled off again, "what the hell were you doing?"

"Someone has to fight this war," he replied.

"Nicht verstehen," I muttered.

I thought Orlando had just been silly and cheeky, but these little things were the beginning. They were the beginning of the fight back. We delivered the beer and I watched Orlando slip a letter or a parcel to the owner at the same time. Something was up but I had no idea what it was.

ACT I, SCENE FIVE
TIME: Summer
1941–Autumn 1942
PLACE: Copenhagen

Apart from the little incidents like the beer
delivery or giving the odd cold shoulder, I don't know
that the family really got involved in any resistance work
in the first year of occupation. I didn't really understand
the politics of it all. I know that in the summer of 1941,
the German leader, Hitler (the one with the funny mustache), whom everyone called the Führer, had gone into
Russia with his men to try and take it over. They had
also declared war on all communists. Danish police
arrested three hundred Danes, including some members
of parliament, for being communists. Some of them
were Jews but that wasn't why they were arrested; in the
beginning it was definitely to do with communism. I
wasn't sure what that was, but I knew from school that
being arrested for what you believe in was against the
Danish constitution. Mrs. Nielsen had taught us that no
Danish citizen could be arrested for his religious or
political beliefs. Our foreign minister, Erik Scavenus,
didn't seem to know this, or he had forgotten, because
he went to Berlin in Germany and signed some deal
with Hitler to stop the communists. To lots of people

this felt like giving in to what the Führer wanted, and some people demonstrated in the streets.

That was when Orlando came home with the black eye.

"It was supposed to be peaceful," he moaned while Mama put a steak on his swelling eyelid. "Then the police came and started beating up people. Can you imagine? Our own police?"

Mama dabbed my brother's eye and then looked at the steak. "Bamse, tell Lisa I think this will still do for supper."

Papa was furious. "I don't want you getting involved, Orlando. You're only sixteen. This is not your fight."

Orlando stood up so quickly that he almost knocked Mama over. "Isn't it, Papa? Then whose fight is it? Why aren't you doing something? What's the matter with you? Why are you just letting this happen? Do you know what the British are calling us? Hitler's Canary! I've heard it on the radio, on the BBC. They say he has us in a cage and we just sit and sing any tune he wants."

I thought Orlando was going to cry but he stormed out of the house while Papa stood clenching his pipe. Mama began to cry and I went to make her a special coffee. We had never had fighting in the house and none of us knew what to say to each other.

Apart from the protests about the communists and the odd bit of trouble in the streets, I don't think it took very long for the Danes to get used to having the Germans under their noses all the time. With the fighting going on in Europe, the Germans were busy, and as long as we were quiet, they pretty much left the Danish people alone. They needed us to grow food and make things in factories. They also needed the Danish trains to get things from Norway and Sweden. Even so, it wasn't long before fuel became scarce. The weather can be very cold in Denmark, and by the autumn of 1942, people were burning furniture or going out into the countryside to dig up peat from the bogs, which they dried and then used for fuel. There were fewer and fewer cars in Copenhagen and soon only those in the "necessary professions"—doctors, ministers, and some journalists—were allowed to buy gasoline. On Saturday nights even people dressed for a party would head out on bicycles. Often they wore wooden clogs with their fancy clothes—there was no leather for shoes, and old socks had to be mended over and over. Mama went through a brief period of being a really good "wife and mother under occupation by enemy forces." I remember her sitting darning a pair of my socks and looking at them under the lamp saying, "I'm sure these have been darned so often there isn't a bit of the original sock left. Look, Bamse, we have made you a completely new sock."

Mama put her hand up the sock and began doing the voice of a glove puppet. Masha and I laughed. None of Mama's domestic good deeds lasted very long.

Everyone took to unraveling old sweaters and reknitting them. Even Mama picked up some needles, and she and Thomas spent hours trying to make "haute couture" out of an old green polo neck and a brown flecked scarf. By now there was no coffee. Mama was a coffee fiend and could not bear any of the many substitutes Papa brought home. She and Thomas would sit pouring rum or whisky or anything on the ground chicory root or grains to make them taste better. It drove my father mad when he caught them.

"Marie, you really shouldn't drink in the middle of the day," he would complain quietly, and Mama would jump like a naughty child.

"Why, Peter, frozen over and in September too."

This was what Mother always said to explain the unexplainable. It had become something of a family joke. She had once been in a production of Harriet Beecher Stowe's story *Uncle Tom's Cabin*. The play was set in the Southern states of America and at one point an escaping slave was supposed to jump off a cliff into the Mississippi River and swim to freedom. One night the stage manager had forgotten to put out the hidden mattress for him to land on and when he jumped he hit the floor with a great thud heard by the entire audience. Undaunted, the actor reappeared from behind the scenery and said, "Frozen over and in September too."

It made Mama laugh every time. Papa was less impressed.

"I mean it, Marie."

"Oh, tell it to the Germans, Peter," Mama continued, sounding deeply offended. "It is not my fault that they have taken away my only vice. I cannot live without coffee," she declared dramatically, as if she might die on the spot.

Thomas would shrug and smile at Papa. "Just trying to make it drinkable, lovey."

Nobody found it easy. Jørgen Johansen, the taxi driver who lived down the road, managed to develop some sort of makeshift engine for his car that ran on cow dung. How many small pieces of the stuff he threw into his contraption depended on where his passenger wanted to go. It had a foul smell and he was forever hanging around Mrs. Jensen's, waiting for the cow to poo so he could go to work. Anton offered to jump on the poor thing again to get her going, but Mrs. Jensen chased him off with her broom. The cab made a clunking sound and Mama said she could smell Johansen coming a mile off.

Having the Germans living with us didn't mean we were protected from the war either. There were frequent air raids, with everyone running to the public underground shelters as soon as the siren went off. Even the sound of the fire engines was terrifying, as it might mean a bomb had exploded nearby.

"Papa, why are they doing this? I thought the British were on our side?" wailed Masha as we all hid under the dining-room table, listening to the sirens and noise outside.

"They are," soothed Papa, "but they have to bomb Danish factories which are working for the Germans. Sssh, it'll be alright. They're not after us."

We knew that the British were on our side. The British radio, the BBC, now broadcast a daily news bulletin in Danish, and it was the only news anyone could rely on. Still, that didn't mean they couldn't hit you by accident, but even with the air raids and the bombs, Mama still went to work. Nothing ever kept her from the theater. In the winter season of '42, she was appearing in a lighthearted revue. Every night the front row was taken by the top German brass, but the show went on. Masha turned sixteen and left school. She got a job at the telephone exchange and suddenly seemed very grown up. We didn't see her much. Everyone knew she had a boyfriend but she wouldn't say who. Orlando was hardly ever home. In addition to his work for Mr. Hansen, he had joined the Union of Danish Youth after attending a lecture by Hal Koch, the professor of church history at the University of Copenhagen. Mr. Koch had toured the country celebrating Danish nationalism, and Orlando had taken every word to heart. He helped to organize outdoor *Alsangs*—community singing of Danish songs—but the Germans soon banned them. Orlando tried to grow a mustache and he got quieter and quieter. He wouldn't let me come on his deliveries for Hansen anymore and he came back late each night. Sometimes he was carrying a parcel or a bunch of papers, but when Papa asked

41

what he was doing, Orlando shook his head and went to his room. I think we all knew he was doing other things, more dangerous things, as well, but no one said anything. Maybe everyone was too scared to ask.

One night the phone rang. Papa hated the telephone. To him it was still a "newfangled invention" and he would shout as if the person on the other end couldn't possibly hear him through a thin piece of wire. I ran to answer before Papa could get up.

"Skovlund," I said as I picked up the phone.

It was a man's voice. A man I didn't know. "Is Orlando there?"

"No," I replied. "Can I take a message?"

"Tell him the sewing club has had to be moved. We'll let him know where."

"Right, and—"

The phone went dead.

Orlando came in after I had gone to bed. I heard him in his room and padded along the hall in my pajamas. He was putting something under his bed and jumped and banged his head when I spoke.

"Bamse! Don't sneak in here like that."

"Sorry. I wasn't sneaking. I had a message. On the phone."

I told him about the sewing club, but he wouldn't tell me what it meant or what was going on.

"You're not old enough. You're only twelve. I don't want you to get involved. It's too dangerous. Now go back to bed."

I couldn't sleep that night. My heart was pounding. How could a sewing club be dangerous? I knew some Danes were already working against the Germans, but I didn't want it to be my brother. I went to sleep thinking about what might be so dangerous and wondering what he was hiding in his room. Orlando and Papa hardly spoke anymore and I didn't really understand it, but I did know one thing: fear, real fear, was beginning to live in our house.

ACT I, SCENE SIX
TIME: September 1942
PLACE: Copenhagen

**As far as I could see,** life for my Jewish friends was the same as before. There were some Danish Nazis who had broken into the synagogue on Krystal Street and tried to burn it down, but everyone I knew thought that was terrible. They were shocked that any Danes could do such a thing. The police had caught them and sent them to prison for three years, but Anton's mother, Mrs. Beilin, could not rest.

"We hold our breath," she would say while she fussed over Gilda, Anton's little sister. "We all just hold our breath."

Gilda was only five and I'm sure she had no idea what her father meant when he said, "We should leave. It is like growing grapes on the slopes of a volcano— as long as it only smokes, you think you can live with the danger. But once the lava comes, it is usually too late to run."

Mr. Beilin had a German accent. He came from Hamburg and it seemed odd to me that he should want to run from his own people.

"You and your volcanoes," scoffed Mrs. B. "You can run. Nineteen thirty-eight we all ran from Hamburg, but I am not going anywhere anymore. This is my home."

Anton would insist, "We're Danes, Papa. You're Danish now. The king will protect us."

Mr. B. would shrug and rub the little black skullcap he wore on his head. "Better to escape once too often than not at all."

"Where is there to run to?" muttered Mrs. B. as she combed Gilda's hair.

I didn't want them to run. I didn't want Anton to go anywhere. We didn't know yet that the German leader, Adolf Hitler, was already putting together the "final solution," his plan to rid Europe of all Jews; that the Nazis were already forcing Jews into concentration camps in the east, where they would be either worked to death or killed in the gas chambers.

Some of Anton's fear was now beginning to be replaced once more by his love of daring exploits. Near our flat there was a main intersection where for some months a German soldier had been directing traffic from behind an island of sandbags. He looked very self-important as he pointed to cars and made them stop while he allowed others to pass by. When he stood behind his wall of sandbags, you could see only his top half. One morning Anton was busy scribbling something on a piece of paper in the hall.

"What are you doing?" I asked, thinking it was some new game.

Anton folded the paper and gave me a large pin to hold. "Come on," he said, grinning, and raced off to get his bike.

I didn't know what was going on but I knew Anton and I knew trouble was brewing. He had that wicked look in his eye. We cycled to the road before the intersection with the sandbag soldier, and Anton parked his bike. The soldier stood in the middle of the crossroads and would turn to face each road in turn as he moved the traffic on. I followed Anton as he snuck down through the shadows from the flats on our left. We got to the crossroads just as the soldier turned to face us, and Anton waved cheerily at him. The soldier ignored him and turned around to direct the next set of traffic. As he did so, Anton shot across the road.

"Come on, Bamse," he called.

I have no idea why I followed him except that I always did. The soldier was now facing away from us. Anton knelt on the road and unfolded his piece of paper.

"Give me the pin," he whispered urgently. I couldn't find the wretched thing in my pocket, and when at last I did, the soldier was about to turn back in our direction. Anton jammed the pin into the paper so that it hung on the sandbags, and we ran for our lives back to the street corner. Puffing and panting, Anton ordered, "Act casual. Look relaxed."

We leaned against a lamppost and waved to the soldier. It was only then that I saw what Anton had written on the paper:

Attention! This soldier is not wearing trousers!

It was kid's stuff, but we could see all the people passing in their cars laughing and the soldier looking more and more confused. Anton and I shook hands in delight, our shoulders shaking. It was a mission well done and we were very pleased with ourselves. Still laughing, we turned back to get our bikes and walked straight into my brother.

Orlando happened to be on one of his deliveries and he had seen the whole thing. I thought he would find it funny too, but he was furious. He grabbed us both by our collars.

"What the hell are you doing?"

Anton tried to wriggle free. I could see he was cross too.

"Let go, Orlando. We were just trying to help. We want to do something too, you know, but everyone says we're too young."

Orlando let go and looked at us both. "You cannot play at this. We are at war," he said.

"I know," replied Anton, "so give us something useful to do."

Anton and Orlando looked so serious: my tiny friend and my great big brother, both ready to fight—

but not each other. I hadn't realized until then that Anton wanted to do something other than play a joke. We had always just had fun.

Playing a joke. That was how Anton and I first started fighting back, and pretty soon we realized that Orlando was right. It wasn't funny at all.

I can remember the date because so much happened on September 15, 1942. I can write about it all now, but at the time we could hardly even whisper what we got up to. After the incident with the traffic soldier, Orlando took me and Anton off to the cellar in our block of flats. It was dark and dripping with damp. No one went down there except to get an old suitcase when they were planning a journey. These days no one even visited relatives in the country, so the place was full of cobwebs.

By now the Germans had been in Denmark for nearly three years. Anton was thirteen and I was twelve and a half. I supposed we were beginning to see things in a different light. I had begun to hate seeing German soldiers casually walking the streets of Copenhagen as if they owned them; eating in the best restaurants and sitting in the front row at Mama's theater. Orlando was just eighteen, and as we sat in the half dark of the cellar, I noticed that his mustache was quite full now and his shoulders were broad. My brother had turned into a man and, more importantly, a man who trusted me.

"I belong to something called BOPA—the *Borgerlige Partisanar*, or Civil Partisans," he began. "It is what is known as an 'underground' resistance group. Do you understand what that means?"

I knew it didn't just mean meeting in cellars, but Anton was straight onto it.

"Secret work fighting the Germans." He was excited. I could see the gleam in his eye and I had a feeling we were about to get involved in things that were a little more daring than jumping on a cow or pinning up notices. I was scared and wanted to run, but Anton was leaning forward, ready to take instruction, and Orlando looked so trusting that I didn't feel I could move. This was my brother and my best friend talking about important matters. I wanted to run to Papa but I knew he wouldn't approve, so I just sat there, shaking inside with a mix of fright and excitement.

Orlando nodded and kept his voice low. "That's right. The BOPA have to be secret about our work. We are quietly fighting the German occupation."

"Like the Churchill Club," cried Anton excitedly.

"Ssh!" snapped my brother, slapping his hand over Anton's mouth. "You have to learn to be quiet." He let go of Anton, who mumbled an apology and pulled his knees up to his chest while Orlando continued in a whisper.

"Yes, like the Churchill Club."

I had seen pictures of the club in the papers. In the spring of 1942, eleven teenage boys had been arrested for belonging to a club that committed small acts of sabotage. They were aged fourteen to seventeen and they called themselves the Churchill Club. I saw their pictures when they were convicted for stealing weapons, setting fire to railroad cars, and putting sugar in the gas tanks of German cars. They seemed very brave. One of them had said to the judge, "If you older folk will do nothing, we will have to do something instead." I wondered if I would ever have such courage, and Orlando was about to put it to the test.

"Now, you could help us with something," he began, and outlined the plan. My big brother trusted me, and my best friend seemed to have no worries about getting involved. I was scared to death but I didn't feel I ever had a choice.

The most popular place in Copenhagen for the top German officers was a restaurant in the center of town called La Tosca. It was always full of soldiers eating and drinking lots of Danish schnapps. Orlando sometimes made deliveries there, and he knew that, after living in Denmark for some time, the Germans had become very relaxed. When they arrived at the restaurant, they used to hang up their jackets in the hallway. Quite often they hung their gun belts there too.

Orlando took me and Anton to the entrance. Inside, we could hear the men laughing as they called out for more drinks.

"Right, Bamse, you go and chat with the soldiers," instructed my brother.

"Why just me?" I asked, thinking I would sooner have had another go at pinning up funny messages.

"So I can get one of their guns," whispered Orlando. "Anton, you wait out here."

"Why can't Anton come in with me?" I inquired. Orlando had said we would both do resistance work. This didn't seem like both of us at all.

Orlando paused and looked a bit embarrassed. "Anton's . . . his . . . his hair is too dark."

I looked at Anton. With his gray, flat cap, you could hardly see his hair at all. Anyway, what did hair matter?

"I want to do something," said Anton, defiantly putting his hands on his hips. "It was my idea we get involved in the first place."

Orlando sighed. "OK, OK. Anton you stand guard at the door and let me know if any police come. Now go on, Bamse"—he gave me a push in the back—"go and talk to them."

"What about?" I was becoming panicky. "What shall I talk to them about?"

"I don't know," replied Orlando impatiently. "Ask them about the Wehrmacht."

"I don't know anything about the Wehrmacht."

"Then you'll have lots of questions," said Orlando, pushing me along the corridor and into the smoky room. I swear it was like one of those American Westerns I had seen at the cinema. I almost fell into the place and it all seemed to go silent. The men looked up and eyed me.

"What do you want?" demanded a blond man in German.

"Hello!" I managed, and then for no reason at all, waved rather feebly. The men laughed and one of them waved back. From the corridor behind me I could hear Orlando hissing, "Get on with it!"

"I want to know about the . . ." For a moment I couldn't think of the name for the German army. In a mirror advertising beer, I could see down the corridor to where Anton waited. Orlando was hidden by the coats hanging on the wall, but I knew he was there.

"I mean, I have questions about . . ." I kept checking the corridor in the mirror and the soldiers saw me looking. As one of them glanced at the reflection, I blurted out, "The Wehrmacht!" as if it were too thrilling for words. "I want to know about the Wehrmacht."

"He wants to know about the Wehrmacht," repeated a lieutenant, and then looked at me. "But you are not alone, are you?"

I thought for a minute I was going to be sick on the spot. He knew. He knew what we were doing. Maybe he would shoot me. Maybe he would shoot Orlando. How would I tell Mama that someone had shot Orlando? Of course, if I were dead myself then I couldn't tell her anything and . . .

The soldier gestured toward the front door, where Anton stood pretending to whistle. "Doesn't your friend want to know about the Wehrmacht?"

Now I certainly didn't know what to do. Should I bring Anton in? What was the problem with his hair anyway? Should I say he wasn't interested? But then they might go and get him themselves and find Orlando under the coats. I tried to be casual and, putting my hands in my trouser pockets, I called out, "Anton, come and say hello."

Anton shuffled up the corridor. I realized that the officer was looking intently at him. We had learned enough German in school to understand when he said, *"Sind Sie Jüde?"* Are you Jewish?

There was a long silence. I looked at my friend, and for the first time I realized how much darker haired he was than me. Did that mean he looked Jewish? Might they think I was Jewish? What if they made Anton take off his cap and show his Jewish hat on the back of his head? Could you kill someone just for wearing a hat?

Anton, please don't take off your hat, don't take off your hat, I repeated over and over in my head while I thought about how many different ways there were to die. The silence was awful. Then Anton, good old Anton, laughed and replied, "Jewish? Of course, isn't everybody?"

The group of soldiers looked shocked until the lieutenant suddenly banged his hand down on the table and began to laugh.

"Very good, very good. Isn't everybody? Come, boys, sit down and we shall tell you about the finest fighting force since the Romans marched under Julius Caesar."

And we sat and we talked and all the while I watched Orlando sneak into the corridor, slip a pistol from a holster, and escape.

Anton and I raced home that night, our heads full of German and fear in equal measure. Our hearts were thumping. We had taken part in the resistance! We had helped steal a gun. We weren't just kids any longer.

ACT I, SCENE EIGHT
TIME: *September 1942*
PLACE: *Charlottenlund*

By the time Anton and I had left the Restaurant, Orlando was nowhere to be seen, so I tore back to our apartment, desperate to talk to him. It was half an hour before supper and I knew that Mama would be getting ready for the theater and that Papa would not be home from the paper yet. Orlando was in the conservatory, patting down the earth around one of Mother's plants.

"Where is it?" I panted.

"Where is what?" snapped Orlando, who, along with turning eighteen, had developed an irritating habit of treating me like a child.

"The gun!" I almost shouted with excitement.

Orlando reached out, grabbed me by the collar, and pulled me to him. "Listen, Bamse, there is no gun, right? If you want to help, then the first thing you need to do is learn to shut up."

"You boys all right?" Papa stood in the doorway, looking at us. We hadn't heard him come in.

Orlando put me down and ran a rough hand across my hair. "Just playing."

Papa frowned. "Right, well—Bamse, go and wash your hands for supper. Then go and say hello to Uncle Johann. He's just arrived."

Both Orlando and I groaned out loud. Uncle Johann was not a favorite and his visits never went well.

"Oh, Papa, no. I—" I began, but Papa gave me a look and I scuttled off. I could tell Orlando was in trouble. I went to wash my hands but I left the bathroom door open so I could hear Papa asking questions.

"What is this, Orlando?" I heard a rustle of paper.

"All the boys are putting them up."

"I do not want it on my front door. I will not have you provoking trouble. We don't want to provide any excuse to arrest the Jews, or us for that matter."

Orlando was almost in tears. "Papa, why do you want to be Hitler's Canary? We can't just tweet for him and do nothing for our pride."

"I know you are angry, Orlando, but this is the best way. Don't cause trouble."

I heard Papa crumple up the piece of paper he was holding, throw it into the wastepaper basket, and say they would talk no more about it.

Uncle Johann was pacing about in the drawing room. Although he was Papa's brother, he was nothing like my gentle father, and I think the whole family had all always been slightly scared of him. He lived out in the country in southern Jutland, and when he came to Copenhagen, he always stayed with us. He was a big, bluff man with a bright red face, as if he had always just stepped out of a high wind. As soon as he saw me, he slapped me hard on the back.

"Ah ha! Bamse, my boy. Not growing any bigger then, you little runt? They ever going to make a man of you? You want to come out on the farm with me for a few days—that'll toughen you up."

"Yes, sir," I mumbled, and thanked God when the call came for supper.

Mama's show was at nine so we ate at six. Papa found all mealtimes very trying. Lisa, our housekeeper, had been with us forever. She was a big round woman from the country. She was probably only fifty but she seemed ancient. She also came from southern Jutland and had an accent as thick as the black bread she cut for us. Papa would sit at the head of the table, pressing and pressing the bell under the carpet with his foot to signal that the next course should be served, unaware that Lisa had disconnected it years ago. She served what she wanted when she wanted, and if Papa did manage to complain, then he never understood her reply. As usual, Mama seemed unconcerned and smiled brightly at everyone. That particular evening she was dressed as an Edwardian English gentlewoman. She looked stunning in the candlelight and she knew Uncle Johann was drooling over her because he always did. Even though he was disgusting she seemed to like it, and she had clearly decided to play the great society hostess that evening. We would have a meal with amusing small talk to accompany her delightful outfit.

She sat smiling while we waited for Papa and Orlando, who were arguing in the hall. I could hear Papa being unusually firm.

"He is your uncle. You will sit down and be pleasant."

"Tell me—has everyone had a pleasant day?" Mama inquired with a slight trill as Papa and Orlando took their seats.

"Not as pleasant as the evening," replied Johann and raised his glass to Mama. He was a clumsy man and looked out of place at Mama's elegant table as he swallowed his wine in one gulp and broke bread into crumbs all over the table.

"Brought you kids a duck for dinner. Shot it myself. Right between the eyes." Uncle Johann raised his hands above his head as if holding a rifle.

"Bang!" he exclaimed, and Mama gave a little start.

"Heavens. Poor thing," she remarked quietly.

The bang reminded me of Anton's and my adventure in La Tosca.

"Oh Mama," I burst out, "it was ever so exciting today. Orlando took me to—"

Before I could get any further, Orlando gave me a sound kick under the mahogany dining table.

"Ow!" I cried.

"Bamse, whatever is the matter?" asked Mama.

"Gr-gr-growing pains," I managed as Orlando threatened my shin again.

"So what did Orlando take you to that was so exciting?" asked Papa while he pressed impatiently with his foot at what he thought was the bell. Behind him the rest of us could see Lisa through the small glass pane in the kitchen door. She was simply waiting till my father stopped trying to call her.

"Masha, please go and see what that woman is up to, will you?" requested Papa quietly, trying to be calm. Masha sighed the sigh only sixteen-year-old girls manage for their fathers and went off to the kitchen. Uncle Johann watched her go.

"Hell of a pretty little thing, Peter. You want to keep an eye on her."

Papa ignored his brother and turned calmly to me. "Now, Bamse, what was it—?"

Mama suddenly clapped her hands and squealed with laughter. "Oh, I have such a funny story from last night. Masha, come and hear this!" she called through the kitchen door.

Lisa swung through the door and began serving food in great dollops. Mama didn't seem to notice how the meatballs bounced down onto the plates. She continued her story.

"You know how the Gestapo take all the best seats at the theater—at the front in the stalls? Well, they are always late and make a great noise when they come in to get everyone to look at their uniforms, and they put their shiny black boots up on the stage. So last night Torvald had gone out onstage to do his opening routine when in come all the soldiers; so he waits. He lets them all get settled and then he suddenly puts his arm straight up in the air like that horrible salute they do to the Führer. Well, I was in the wings and I couldn't believe it. Was he going to salute those hideous men? The audience was shocked—you could hear it. Of course, all the Germans leaped to their feet, thrust an arm in the air, and shouted, 'Heil Hitler!' Then they all sat down again, and still Torvald hadn't said a word and was just standing there with his arm in the air. There was a terrible silence and then he turned to the audience and said, 'You know, last winter the snow outside my house was this high.' The Germans were furious and everyone else was crying with laughter."

Papa shook his head. "He shouldn't do it." But he laughed as he said it.

"Very good, very funny," Uncle Johann nodded, helping himself to more wine. "But that doesn't mean we don't have to think about the Jewish problem."

There was a silence. Papa frowned at Orlando but he couldn't leave the matter alone.

"What Jewish problem, Uncle?" asked my brother.

"Come on, Orlando, don't be naïve. Something has to be done about the Jews."

Papa shook his head. "I don't understand you."

His brother looked at him. "The Jews are ruining our businesses. They have to go. It's nothing. What are there? Maybe eight thousand at most." There was silence at the table. Uncle Johann looked at us all. "If we help the Nazis with this, they will leave us alone," he persisted. "Some of my neighbors have joined the Schalburg Corps. It's not a bad idea."

There was a sharp intake of breath from Papa. The Schalburg Corps was a Danish Nazi SS volunteer force. Rumor had it that the Germans used them to terrorize local people into doing whatever was wanted.

"Are you mad? You can't just call people Jews and then throw them out of the country. They're Danes as well," exploded Orlando furiously. "Some of them have been here for centuries. What about the Viking Jews? Christian the Fourth invited Jews here in the seventeenth century, offering them freedom of religion and the right to trade. Frederick the Fourth gave them full equality in eighteen fourteen. They're as Danish as the rest of us."

Mama beamed at Orlando. "That was very good, darling. Wasn't that good, Peter?"

Orlando blushed and looked down at the table.

Papa nodded. "Orlando is right. Johann, there is nothing to be afraid of. No one is going to take anything from you. The Jews have as much right to be here as anyone, but in a way it is not a question of Jews and their rights. It's about us and who we are as a nation. There's never been a ghetto in Denmark. We don't characterize people by religion or anything else. Everything we do is based on equality and human dignity." Papa seemed almost to be pleading with his brother. "Johann, you know that."

Johann snorted. "All I know is that I will be glad when they make them wear the yellow star so at least you can spot them."

Orlando turned to Papa, pleading, "Papa, how can you let him sit here?"

"He's my brother," replied Papa quietly. "You don't understand, Orlando. Johann, can't you—?"

I didn't understand at all. "Uncle Johann," I asked, "if you can't spot them without the yellow star on, then they must just be the same as us. I mean, otherwise you would know them without the star, wouldn't you?"

"I'd know them anyway," mumbled Uncle Johann. "They look different. People shouldn't look so different."

Mama reached out and put her hand on Papa's, but I ploughed on.

"Why are the Germans so afraid of the Jews? My friend Anton is Jewish and he's not scary at all."

Uncle Johann put down his knife and fork with a bang and looked straight at me. "You have a Jewish friend? Peter, how can you let him?"

"I am not going to sit here and listen to this." Orlando threw down his napkin on the table and pushed back his chair so violently that it fell backward on the carpet.

Fortunately, Lisa chose that moment to bring in the duck.

"Sit down, darling," said Mama quietly but firmly, "or we'll all get indigestion."

Orlando glowered at Papa but the smell of the roast duck was probably too much, because he picked up his chair and sat down. The whole table went silent: I think everyone was wondering whether you could still see where it had got Johann's bullet between the eyes. If Johann had had any sense he would have realized that it was a good moment to change the conversation, but he didn't.

"The Jews in Germany wear the yellow star. In fact, they wear it in all the occupied countries and you don't hear them complaining."

"You don't hear them at all," muttered Orlando.

"They say if the Germans bring in the yellow star for the Jews, then the king will wear one," I contributed.

"That old fool," sneered Johann.

"If they make Anton wear one, then I will too," I said, thinking I wouldn't mind at all if he didn't.

"I don't think yellow is a good color for anyone," contributed Mama. "Makes one look so pale. I remember a production of *All's Well* when dear Thomas—"

Suddenly Papa put down his knife and fork. "Where the hell is Masha? I send her to get the dinner and we get the dinner and lose her. What the hell is going on tonight? Masha!"

Masha came stumbling through the door looking bright red and flustered. "Sorry, Papa. I . . . I—"

"All right, all right, sit down. Now let's stop talking about stars and Jews and the color yellow and get on with our dinner."

"Just vegetables for me, Lisa," whispered Mama, clearly still worried about the way the duck had lost its life.

Uncle Johann toasted Mama again with his wine. "Beautiful woman. I never married because I never found anyone as beautiful as Marie. You're a lucky dog, Peter—family, Marie, this home . . ."

He had had quite a bit to drink by now, and when Lisa brought in the dessert, he got to his feet and pretended to chase after her. She escaped shrieking to the kitchen, with Uncle Johann hot on her heels. Everyone was embarrassed.

"'Exit pursued by a bear,'" said Mama, quoting her favorite line of Shakespeare, and we all laughed.

I remember that night. Mama looking so beautiful in the candlelight and Papa sitting at the head of the table. Even Masha and Orlando laughed at one of Mama's stories, and Papa held her hand while they drank their coffee. Uncle Johann was right about something. We were lucky.

ACT I, SCENE NINE
TIME: *September 1942*
PLACE: *Charlottenlund*

Mama went to work, and Uncle Johann, who
had had too much wine, fell asleep in his chair at the
dining table. Before I went to bed, I snuck out to the
conservatory and pulled out Orlando's piece of paper
that Papa had thrown away.

TEN COMMANDMENTS FOR DANES

1. You must not go to work in Germany
   or Norway.

2. You shall do a bad job for the Germans.

3. You shall work slowly for the Germans.

4. You shall destroy important machines and tools.

5. You shall destroy everything that may be of
   benefit to the Germans.

6. You shall delay all transport.

7. You shall boycott German and Italian films
   and papers.

8. You must not shop at Nazis' stores.

9. You shall treat traitors for what they are worth.

10. You shall protect anyone chased by the Germans.

JOIN THE STRUGGLE FOR
THE FREEDOM OF DENMARK!

I thought it sounded wonderful. My brother was so brave and I felt I would do anything for him, just as I had helped in the restaurant. I wanted to tell him so, there and then, but he and Papa were arguing again in the kitchen.

"Orlando, you don't understand," Papa was saying. "I worry about you. You're my son. I don't want you to get hurt."

"What happened to you, Papa?" Orlando sounded desperate. "Where is the man who draws political cartoons?"

Papa shook his head. "I don't know. Maybe that was a mistake. What is the point of thumbing my nose at the Germans if I lose my job and can't feed my family? I've been through times with no food before. You wouldn't understand. Things are bad. Prices are very high. We need to eat."

"Prices are high because the Germans are here and they take everything," Orlando answered in a deep voice. I suddenly realized that my brother also sounded like a man. A very determined man. "Papa, we have to fight. We have a duty as Danes. Think of our history. We were the first European nation to grant the Jews full, unconditional emancipation. We were the first country to abolish slavery officially. We can't give in now."

"We need stability, Orlando," Papa answered wearily. "Yes, we did all those things, but Denmark is a tiny nation. We can't fight our enemies. We haven't the strength. They won't take the Jews or anyone as long as we cooperate. The Germans will leave us and the Jews alone as long as they are not provoked."

There was a long silence until at last Orlando said, "And who would they have to take before you decided to do something about it, Papa?"

Papa didn't answer. I heard Orlando going quietly into the hall to fetch his coat. Papa called after him but his words echoed against Orlando's footsteps on the stairs. Then there was silence, broken only by Uncle Johann snoring in his dining chair as his head rested next to the salt and pepper.

I didn't hear Papa come into the conservatory. I was still holding the commandments in my hand when he came up behind me.

"Oh, Bamse," he said, looking at the crumpled paper, "not you too."

I thought Papa was going to cry and I didn't want him to, but I felt fired up by what Orlando had said.

"I'm sorry, Papa, but I think Orlando is right."

My voice trembled as I spoke and I felt afraid when Papa slumped down on a chair and held his head in his hands.

"Of course you do. He is your big brother. Come here."

He pulled me to him the way he used to when I was tiny. I sat on his lap and he stroked my head.

"You know, Bamse, people are never as straight-forward as you might think. Orlando wants to fight because he is young and Uncle Johann is afraid because he is old."

"I don't understand," I said, still inspired by Orlando. "I mean, Papa, Orlando says—"

Papa put his finger on my lips to shush me and began to tell me a story.

"When I was a boy—about your age—I used to make model airplanes," he began. "We lived in the country, on a farm, and I thought it was boring. I wanted to be a pilot. I had seen only one airplane. It landed in a field one summer when the pilot got lost and stopped to ask the way. I thought it was the most wonderful thing I had ever seen. Every afternoon I worked on little engines and wooden wings. It was autumn and the barn was full of the hay my father and Johann had worked so hard to bring in from the fields. It was enough to last us the winter and it smelled wonderful. I couldn't get one of my planes to take off properly, so I took it up into the hayloft in the barn to give it some height. I had been told a million times not to play in there, but I didn't listen. The barn was lit by oil lamps and the soft light shone on my model plane—it was a little beauty. It looked almost real as it took off from the loft, but I lost control of it and it flew straight into one of the lamps. There was a tinkling of glass and the flame seemed to leap to the plane. It caught fire and flew on another meter or so, straight into one of the bales of hay."

I looked at Papa's face. His eyes were gazing into the distance as if he were still in the barn.

"I tried to put it out but the flames leaped so fast from one part of the barn to the other. Before I knew it, the fire was raging across the doors and I couldn't get out. I tripped and fell. The next thing I knew, I was lying on the ground in the yard. My brother, your uncle Johann, was kneeling over me, crying, and the barn was ablaze. He was the only one at home. He had been told to watch me, and when the fire started he knew I was in there. He risked his life to pull me out."

I reached up and stroked the red mark that stained the side of Papa's face. "Is that how you got the mark on your face?" I asked.

Papa nodded. "I was badly burned, but not as badly as the barn. No one could stop the fire, and it kept on till there was nothing but ash. It was a terrible winter, with no food for the animals and all of us depending on the kindness of our neighbors. My father hated it, but, do you know, no one in the family ever said a word to me about it. My father just said he was so glad not to lose me as well. My mother cried a lot but it was worst for your Uncle Johann. He had such nightmares about pulling me from the fire.

He would cry in the night and wake up calling my name. He risked his life for me, and I think he has been afraid ever since. He was ashamed that he had not watched over me; that he hadn't saved the barn as well. Then, when I went to school, the kids teased me. I looked so different from everyone else. So many times Johann defended me when others called me names or laughed. I think now he can't bear it if anyone looks just a bit different. Don't judge your uncle too harshly. I wouldn't be here at all if it hadn't been for him."

Papa hugged me tight. "Life is never straightforward. Maybe the grown-ups are more fearful than you know, Bamse. It is easier to be brave when you are young. I feel about you the way my father did for me. I don't want you or Orlando to get hurt. Stay away from the burning barn, my son."

With that Papa kissed me and stood up. He took a blanket off the end of the chair and I watched him go into the dining room. Carefully he wrapped the blanket around his brother's shoulders and then turned out the light.

I went to bed in my tiny box room, my head reeling from everything I had been told. I didn't know whether to fight or not fight; whether to follow my brother or my father. I felt as if there was a war going on in my own head. I was debating all these things when I thought I heard something. My room looked down onto the yard, and I peeked out behind the

Mørklægningsrullegardiner—blackout curtains—which we all had so that the British RAF didn't bomb us by mistake.

I thought maybe the noise was Mrs. Jensen's cow, but down below someone lit a cigarette and as he shook the match to blow it out, he looked up. It was one of the "green ones"—that's what everyone called the German soldiers—one of the green ones standing right there in our yard. I crawled under the covers. What should I do? Why was he in our yard? Maybe he was just having a cigarette. He didn't look that old. Almost human. Could all the green ones turn into monsters overnight? Was he watching the house? Did he know about the pistol? Should I tell someone?

Mama had gone to the theater and, as usual, Orlando had gone out. I tried to think what to do. Papa said we shouldn't do anything to provoke the German authorities. Don't give the Nazis an excuse to arrest Jews, Papa had said. Could you provoke a German if you asked him to get out of your yard? Would he rush up and arrest Anton and his mom and dad? Would he arrest me? I felt ashamed that I was afraid. I had been afraid in the restaurant: afraid that the Germans would think I was Jewish; afraid for myself instead of for my friend. I was about to go and get my father when I saw the kitchen door open. It was my sister, Masha. She came out into the yard and went over to the soldier, who put his arms around her. For a second I thought she was looking up, so I sat back down on my bed and let the curtain fall across the window. I didn't know what to do. I didn't want Papa to get into trouble, but I knew Masha was doing something wrong. I decided to do nothing and I felt ashamed. I turned my head to my pillow and for the first time since war had come to Denmark, I began to cry.

ACT II, SCENE ONE
TIME: *September 1942*
PLACE: *Copenhagen*

**By September of 1942** the king, the man my
uncle thought was an old fool, was himself causing
trouble. No one had asked the Jews or the king or anyone else to walk the streets wearing the yellow star of
David, but that didn't mean there weren't problems. The
prime minister, Vilhelm Buhl, had been on the radio
asking all Danes to stop committing acts of sabotage
against the Germans. I think that, like Papa, he didn't
want anyone to provoke our occupiers out of the calm.

A lot of the protests were small. Many people,
including my mother, had started wearing four coins
tied together with ribbons in the red and white of the
Danish flag in their buttonholes. Danish coins have
holes in the middle and the four coins added up to
nine *øre* (just a few pennies), which represented the
date of the occupation, April 9. The Germans knew
what the ribbons meant but there was nothing they
could do about them.

Nor could they do anything about the V campaign, which was soon everywhere you looked. A man
called Leif Grundel, speaking Danish on the BBC, had

started the V campaign in 1941—*Vi Vil Vinde*. It meant "we will win." Soon there were *V*s everywhere—on walls, in advertisements, even in white paint on the side of German cars. "V for Victory" said the British, and they began using the music from Beethoven's Fifth Symphony, which starts like Morse code—dot, dot, dot, dash—the sound of the letter *V*.

We had also heard more and more stories about ordinary people doing extraordinary things, like blowing up railway tracks. Prime Minister Buhl asked people to report sabotage of any kind to the police. Orlando was furious and after that he would listen only to the BBC. He said you couldn't trust anyone: even his own prime minister was guilty of treason.

On September 26 it was the king's birthday. He was seventy-two and there were Danish flags out everywhere to celebrate. It seems that Mr. Hitler sent him a long telegram wishing him "Happy Birthday" over and over, and lots of other nice things. Well, the king was not thrilled by this and just sent back a note saying, "My utmost thanks, Christian Rex," which I thought covered everything he needed to say. It was just the sort of note my mother made me write when Great-aunt Signe sent me those itchy vests she made. Anyway, that was how the "Telegram Crisis" started. Hitler was furious, so he sent someone new to be in charge of Denmark. By now the BBC were telling us that things weren't going well for the Germans, and I guess they weren't about to lose us too. A Gestapo SS man called

Dr. Werner Best arrived as the new high commandant of Denmark. I think everyone knew that things were about to turn ugly. Everyone except, of course, Mama.

The season had finished at the theater and for the moment there were no new shows. One Saturday Mama was up quite early.

"I think I will go to Sallie Besiakov's and order a new hat. Who wants to take a trip to Amager?"

"I'm busy," said Masha, who seemed rather dressed up for a Saturday morning. She gave Mama a quick kiss and was out the door.

"I can go," said Papa.

Mama looked confused. "But you'll be at work."

He shook his head. "No. There are to be no more cartoons at the paper. They have been forbidden."

There was a brief pause. So Papa had lost his job, just as he had predicted. I could see the look in his eyes. The family barn was on fire but I don't think Orlando knew that. He and Papa hardly spoke anymore, but now he got to his feet and exploded, "You see! Why don't you admit it, Papa, no Danish papers can be trusted anymore. They are full of Nazi propaganda and lies. No one is allowed to print the truth."

Papa stood wearily and walked over to Orlando. He placed a hand on his eldest son's shoulder, but Orlando shook it off. There was a moment's pause while Mama poured some coffee.

"How will we live?" she asked, as if inquiring if it might rain.

"I'll paint some portraits, I'll do some work at the theater—we'll be fine," soothed Papa.

"No one wants portraits. We're living in a city where taxis run on cow dung, for goodness' sake. You shouldn't have provoked them with your elephant drawings."

"No. No, I shouldn't."

"They were brilliant, Papa," said Orlando, looking at Papa with pride.

"You could write for the underground," I said quietly. "Orlando says—"

"Shut up, Bamse," said Orlando.

Papa looked at us both and sighed. "I hear there might be work at the theater in Århus doing some designs."

Papa left on the train for Århus the next day, telling us not to get into trouble. The town was a day's journey away by train and ferry and he would be gone for some weeks. It was odd not having him around, and I know Mama missed him very much.

Everything was changing, yet some things stayed the same. There were berries on the rowan trees now and that meant school had started again. Orlando now had Anton and me busy doing little jobs for the resistance from the moment we came out of school. Mama didn't seem to notice what we were up to, but one day she came back in a terrible state.

"Oh children, I can't believe I am home. I thought we were going to die."

You could never really tell with Mama which bit was theater and which was real life, but this time it seemed real enough. She was hysterical, and without Papa there no one knew what to do. Masha ran to get Thomas from the theater while Orlando tried to find out where she had been. Mama paced around and seemed unable to calm down. I had never seen her in such a state and it was scary. I tried to get her to sit down and went to find a stool for her feet but she wouldn't settle.

"I only went to Sallie Besiakov's shop to collect my new hat," she half sobbed. "Just the hat shop in Amager. Amager, for God's sake! Nothing ever happens in Amager. Even the tram can hardly be bothered to go there. Just going to get a hat. That was all. Not doing any harm to anyone."

"Mama, you have to calm down," pleaded Orlando. He tried to put his arms around her but she pulled away. Tears were running down her face and ruining her makeup, something Mama never allowed to happen.

"Who the hell are the Hitler Jugend?" she demanded.

Orlando looked at her sharply. "Why?"

"I was inside the shop chatting with Sallie, who is so charming—such a nice hat; she had been waiting for those ostrich feathers—and then these louts suddenly appeared. First they started scraping marks all over the window of the shop, and then they started chanting nasty words about Jews, and Sallie was so shocked. They were banging on the window and making such ugly faces. Sallie locked the door but the glass cracked—it was just the two of us and we couldn't get out—"

"Who are they, Orlando?" I asked.

"A Danish Nazi youth group," he replied. All the muscles in his jaw had tightened. The fight seemed to be getting nearer and nearer and I could sense that this was just the beginning of trouble ahead.

"Sallie never did anything to anyone. At last the police came, but those horrid young people just ran away. It was all I could do to get on the tram and—Oh . . . Thomas!"

The front door opened and Mama's beloved Thomas arrived, fussing about with bottles of liniment and bits of silk scarf.

"It's all right, Marie, I am here now." He put his arm around her and led her away.

"Oh Thomas, the shop is ruined and Sallie—I don't know what will happen to Sallie . . . ," wailed Mama. Thomas made clucking and soothing noises and locked Mama and himself in her bedroom. We knew they would be in there for hours.

Masha and I turned to Orlando. With Papa away, Orlando was the man of the family now.

He didn't seem to know what to say. None of us had ever seen Mama quite so bad.

"Well . . ." Orlando cleared his throat. "Well, it's up to us. We have to try to get on as normally as possible. Masha, you go and see if Lisa—"

"I'm going out," declared Masha, fetching her coat.

"Masha!" said Orlando, trying to be stern, but it was too late. The front door banged shut on Masha's exit. There was an eerie silence in the flat, broken only by the odd sob from Mama's bedroom and the sound of Thomas singing quietly.

"We are working in 'Norwegian conditions,' you know," Orlando muttered to me.

I nodded even though I didn't really know what it meant. I guessed it was just being part of the fight. In Norway the resistance actually fought the Germans openly, and I knew Orlando wanted us to do the same but I was scared. Papa wasn't there, and Mama had fallen apart. I was sure Orlando was doing dangerous things and, worst of all, I knew Masha had a secret and I hadn't told anyone.

Anton's mom and dad, Mr. and Mrs. Beilin, had a radio. It was a great big wooden box about half a meter long, with ivory tuning dials. Our family had never had one because Mama said that if people wanted entertainment, they should go to the theater. One of the jobs Orlando had given me and Anton was to tune in to the BBC news every evening and take notes about what they had said. This wasn't easy as we didn't have very much English, so Mrs. Beilin would sit with us and translate. She knew it was necessary, but the whole business made her very anxious.

"Turn it right down," she would say as her hands crumpled and uncrumpled the apron around her waist. I could see she was worried to death in case anyone overheard. The Germans had made it illegal to listen, so we used to sit with our heads almost glued to the wooden box. I hated the look of fear on Mrs. Beilin's face. The world had turned upside down: grown-ups were supposed to tell you everything was all right, not look scared themselves. Anton and I sat on one side of the set and Mrs. B. sat with Gilda on her lap on the other. In the beginning Mr. Beilin had joined us, but lately he didn't seem well. More and more he just sat in a corner and hardly said a word. I thought of him sitting on the slopes of his volcano.

"You don't know," he would murmur. "You don't know what they can do. We should go. We should leave." But he didn't look as if he had the energy to go anywhere or do anything. I used to see him going out to the synagogue to teach Hebrew, but by the winter of 1942, he had stopped leaving the flat at all. Anton said that his dad was turning into a ghost.

Some nights Mrs. Beilin brought in ginger cookies and glasses of milk from Mrs. Jensen's cow. Jørgen Johansen was feeding her so much grass now to get her to poo for his taxi that there was plenty of milk as well. Mrs. Beilin would look at her husband and shake her head.

"He was a writer, you know, my husband . . . in Germany. A brilliant writer. But then they stopped all that. Nineteen thirty-three—all the Jews in Germany were stopped from working for newspapers, magazines, radio stations, or anything to do with films or the theater," she tutted to herself. "We weren't even allowed to be teachers or farmers."

I didn't understand it. Why farmers? Mrs. Jensen's cow couldn't even tell which yard she lived in let alone what religion her owner was.

"It was terrible. Lots of German shops had signs that said JEWS STRICTLY FORBIDDEN, and if you lived in a small town, it had become difficult to get food. They stopped the kids from going to school, and we all had to carry special identification papers and have our passports marked with a *J*—*Jude*, the German for Jew."

I looked at Anton, who had heard the stories a million times. This was my friend and I wondered what I could do to protect him. I didn't want to hear about everyone being afraid. I was having enough trouble being brave without worrying about the adults around me. There seemed to be fear in every room.

"Everyone was scared," said Mrs. B. "Not just the Jews. There was so little money and work and it was easy to blame the Jews. It was what Hitler told them to do, but that night . . . *Kristallnacht*—the night of broken glass—November the ninth, nineteen thirty-eight . . . the synagogues burned, Jews were thrown from trains and buses, humiliated and beaten, people were killed, cemeteries were vandalized and destroyed, can you imagine? They even hated our dead. Our homes were broken into and looted and thousands of businesses went up in flames while the German fire brigade stood by and watched. And all the while the German police did nothing—some even helped . . . and the thousands, thousands who were taken east . . ."

I didn't know what that meant. To be taken east. It was obviously bad and could not be allowed to happen here. I looked at my friend and wondered if Anton would be taken east. Could you visit someone in the east? Did anyone come back from there?

"How did you get to Denmark?" I asked.

"My sister Elsa—you met her, the one from Hellerup—she was a member of the Danish Women's League for Peace and Freedom. They helped us escape over the German border and into Denmark." Mrs. Beilin sighed. "We never thought we might have to do it again." The news came on and Mrs. B. began to cry quietly.

Her stories made Anton and me concentrate all the harder on the job we had been given. We wrote down everything that was said on the radio. That way, if the Germans claimed they had won a battle in the Soviet Union or North Africa and the BBC said they hadn't, we could pass on the truth.

At first we just took our scribbled paper to a street corner outside the bicycle shop. Orlando would tell us to wait for a man with such and such a color shirt or jacket or a particular hat. We would wait and when the man or woman appeared we would hand over the paper without saying anything and then just walk away.

Trying to find out the truth about the war in Europe was very important. Everyone was printing underground newspapers. It was the best way to spread news and it didn't seem to matter what your politics were. Even the communists and the conservatives printed papers together—papers with names like *Free Denmark* (*Frit Danmark*) and *Land and People* (*Land og Folk*). Soon we got to know who the couriers were and they began to trust us. Anton and I had learned how to keep quiet. Even Orlando realized that we could keep a secret now.

One day he took us to the place where one of the papers was being printed. It was a dentist's office and it looked strange. The place was full of men in shirt-sleeves working with trays of printing type on their laps. All the dentist's equipment was covered in bits of paper and blocks of ink as they hurried to get the next newsletter ready. Bits of paper with more information, or even jokes and cartoons, would turn up at the door marked for the attention of the dentist, and the men were endlessly making last-minute changes before the press started. One sheet of paper would be printed; then the dentist would start up his drill, which would drown out the clanging noise as the papers churned out of a duplicating machine.

Sometimes the copies were done on very light, thin paper. I watched a businessman arrive in his suit and tie. He took one of these lightweight papers and rolled it very thin, as if making a cigarette. Then he took a pen from his inside pocket and pulled it apart. The paper went in the place for the ink cartridge. He never said a word but put the pen back into his jacket and left. Orlando saw me looking.

"He goes to Sweden. He has permission for his work. He will get the paper to Britain, to the BBC."

Incredible. Anton and I listened to the BBC and now we were helping send news to them in London.

All over Copenhagen the same thing was going on. One person might write something, then give it to a man on a street corner; he would pass it to another to publish; then it went to another to distribute. Often none of them would meet, but the news always got out. I never went there, but they said there was even a paper printed in the subbasement of the Dagmarhus, where the Nazis had their headquarters. I would love to have seen that.

Soon Orlando had other jobs for me and Anton. I had stopped trying to blurt out what we were up to each day and he had started to trust me. Not that there was anyone to tell. Papa was still away, Masha was hardly ever home, and Mama had drifted off into a world of her own where no one could reach her. She had seen enough in Amager to know that she didn't want to get involved. It didn't matter: I knew I had work to do. Somehow Mr. Beilin's silence at home had made it all real to me. This wasn't a game. It wasn't just some idea. It was about protecting Anton and his mom and dad and Sallie, the hat-shop lady in Amager whose grandfather had made hats for the Cossacks.

ACT II, SCENE THREE
TIME: *December 1942*
PLACE: *Copenhagen*

___"Right,"___ ___said___ ___my___ ___brother___ one early evening
just before Christmas as the duplicating machine
whirred beside the dentist's drill. "I have a new job for
you. It isn't easy but you're small and I think you'll be
perfect for it." Orlando explained what we had to do,
and Anton and I nodded. I have no idea why we just
nodded. I'm sure we were both terrified, but we never
talked about it. Everyone was so frightened that there
was no point in discussing it.

That evening as darkness fell, Anton and I cycled
down to Hovedbanegården—Copenhagen's main
railway station. As usual it was busy with commuters
going out to the suburbs. There were patrols of German soldiers, but no one really seemed to be on their
guard. Certainly no one thought anything of two
schoolboys come down to look at the trains. We did
exactly what Orlando had told us.

As usual Anton led the way. "You carry the notebook," he said, thrusting a small pad and a pen into my
hand. "Now, pretend to write down the names and

model numbers of the different engines," he instructed as we wandered along the platforms.

He waved to a couple of passing green uniforms.

"Don't do that," I hissed. I always felt that Anton went that bit too far.

"Why not?" He grinned at me.

"It draws attention to us," I muttered, writing down another number.

"Exactly," replied Anton, pulling his cap low over his eyes. "No one will think we are up to something if we've drawn attention to ourselves." He waved again because he knew it annoyed me. It was typical. He always had to be that bit more bold than me.

Moving down the platforms at last, we arrived at the terminus for the boat trains, which the Germans used for sending freight from Denmark to Sweden. Lots of people were loading boxes, and there were trolleys of stuff being pushed to and fro.

"Now," whispered Anton, "I'm smallest, so you keep writing and I'll do the newsletter."

"Have you got the tape?" I asked for the twentieth time.

Anton looked shocked and clapped his hands on his pockets. "Oh no, I forgot it!" he exclaimed.

"Anton!"

He pulled a roll of tape out of his pocket and laughed. "Will you stop worrying? I've got everything."

Even though there was snow on the ground and a chill in the air, I could feel sweat trickling down my back. Anton and I had spent so many hours playing at being spies and cowboys, but this was too real. I didn't like it at all.

We checked the platform and when no one was looking, Anton slipped down onto the track and under one of the railroad cars. He had with him a copy of the newsletter, which he was to tape to the underneath of the carriage. Once the train got to Sweden, a member of the resistance there would find it and pass on the news. Sweden was neutral in the war, so there was no danger for anyone there, but it was different for us. I stood scribbling intently as a German guard sauntered over to me. He looked like my Uncle Johann: middle-aged and a bit fat. Lots of the green ones looked like that. They were either quite old and fat or very young and thin. I guess if they had been something in the middle, Hitler would have used them for actual fighting. This one was smoking a cigarette and puffed a great balloon of smoke in my face as he stood in front of me.

"Collecting train numbers?" he asked.

"Yes, yes, I am," I said in slow German.

"I did that when I was a boy," he replied.

I nodded. "Did you . . . did you . . . get any interesting ones?" I managed, praying he wouldn't ask to look in my notebook, which was almost entirely blank.

The man was about to tell me a story—perhaps of a fascinating encounter with a fast express to Switzerland—when Anton's head suddenly appeared at the edge of the platform. The soldier and I spotted him at the same moment.

"Hey!" yelled the man. "What's he doing down there?"

I grabbed Anton's arm and pulled him up. "He dropped his notebook," I shouted over my shoulder as we began to run.

Anton grinned and yelled, "Don't worry. It was empty anyway."

"You come back here!" shouted the German, starting after us, but he was too big to follow for long.

Anton and I leaped on our bikes and didn't look back until we were home. We leaned against the walls of our yard, panting and panting as if our hearts would burst.

"Do you think . . . ," managed Anton between huge gulps of air, "that those were Norwegian conditions?"

I nodded. "Oh yes, those were definitely Norwegian."

ACT II, SCENE FOUR
TIME: *December 1942*
PLACE: *Charlottenlund*

**My heart was so full** of adrenaline and excitement that I thought I would explode if I didn't tell someone, but when I got in, the flat was silent. Mama and Orlando were sitting in the drawing room. Papa was home. I might be a big resistance fighter now but that didn't mean I couldn't run and throw myself into his arms.

"Papa, you're home. Oh, we missed you."

He looked tired and pale as he hugged me close. "Hello, my boy. Did you think I could miss Christmas with you? I have a present for you, Bamse, but first I just need to talk to your mother and Orlando. You go to your room for a minute."

Orlando reached out to stop me. "No, it's OK, Papa, Bamse has done more than you know."

Mama was wearing black, so I knew the conversation was to be serious.

"While I was in Århus," explained Papa, "a ship docked from Norway. Everyone knew what it was." He rubbed his eyes. He looked shattered. "The Germans have arrested all the Norwegian Jews. There were five hundred and thirty of them, and they were on their way to a concentration camp at a place called Auschwitz. Everyone in Århus knew. There they were, in a Danish harbor, and none of us could do anything about it. Those poor people down in the hold of that boat like cattle. I felt so helpless." Papa turned to my brother. "I was wrong, Orlando. I thought we could just sit it out, but we have to do something." He looked at Mama, who was sitting silently. "Marie, you cannot talk about this to anyone."

We all looked at Mama. Keeping quiet about anything was not what she did best.

Mama clasped her hands to her breast in horror at our looks. "Oh boys, for goodness' sake. There are no secrets except the secrets that keep themselves and surely this . . . you know"—Mama waved airily about her—"is . . . well, one of those."

"George Bernard Shaw," said Papa.

"Well, maybe," replied Mama with a sniff, "but true nonetheless. Oh, my lovely boys." She gathered us all to her as she declared, "Life is either a daring adventure or nothing. To keep our faces towards change and behave like free spirits in the presence of fate is strength undefeatable."

Papa patted her cheek. "Helen Keller."

Mama rose, slightly offended. "I was brilliant as that poor deaf, blind woman. Now then . . . a resistance outfit." She drifted off to her bedroom, calling over her shoulder, "Orlando, is there a particular color everyone is wearing?"

So now the whole family was going to be in the resistance. I felt a great surge of pride—as if Mr. and Mrs. Beilin were as good as saved. I wanted to rush off and tell Anton.

"We must tell Masha," said Papa. Masha. I hadn't thought about Masha and her friend in green.

"Papa—" I began, but then the doorbell sounded, and we could hear Lisa shuffle off to open it. Even though we had done nothing, the three of us froze.

"Merry Christmas, my family. More ducks and half a pig this time," we heard from the corridor. It was the unmistakable voice of Uncle Johann.

"Merry Christmas!" he boomed. "I'm back and you'll be pleased to know this time it's for good."

Now that the whole family—except, of course, Uncle Johann—was going to get involved in the resistance, I knew that I had to speak to my sister. Most nights I had seen her slip out into the yard to meet the young German soldier, and I knew it was wrong. I also knew Orlando would kill her if he found out. One morning we met just as she was coming out of the bathroom. With one extra staying in the flat, getting time in the bathroom was becoming more and more difficult.

"Masha? Could I have a word?" I began.

"What is it, squirt?" Masha never had much time for me, so I wasn't surprised by her tone.

"It's about 'Fritz.'"

"Fritz who?"

"Well, I don't know what his name is. It probably isn't Fritz, but you know it might be and anyway—"

Masha grabbed my arm and pulled it up behind my back. "Listen, Bamse, I don't know what you're talking about, but just keep your nose out of my business, OK?"

"But Masha!"

"Just mind your own business or I'll kill you."

Now I was stuck. Obviously, I didn't want Masha to kill me, but then I didn't want the Germans to do that either. Maybe the guy she was going out with was one of the nice young ones. Maybe I should just wait a little and see. Maybe I was still a coward.

Meanwhile, Papa began writing and doing cartoons for the underground paper, and Anton and I carried on doing whatever jobs we were asked to. I'm not sure what Mama did for the resistance, because a new production of *The Seagull* went into rehearsals and most days she was out at the theater. When she came home, she was tired. She would stroke my face and say, "Women can't forgive failure."

You might have thought she was trying to encourage me in our fight, but I knew it was just a quote from the play. I am ashamed to tell you that at that time, I doubted whether Mama would ever do anything really helpful. In fact, I began to think the theater was rather a waste of time.

Meanwhile, Uncle Johann would go out in the evenings, but in the day he never seemed to leave the flat. We knew he had come to help organize the Schalburg Corps, the Danish Nazis, in Copenhagen, but Papa said that if we told him to leave, there would only be trouble; that we should just pretend to get on with our lives. It must have been difficult for my father. Uncle Johann was his big brother: I wondered how I would feel if Orlando wasn't on our side. Of course, keeping things quiet from my uncle meant that now we had secrets in our own home as well as in the streets.

Orlando had started university, and straight away he began to train in the Deer Park with members of the University Rifle Club. He was obsessed with getting hold of what he called "perforating machines," by which he meant any kind of gun. The BBC told us that the war in Europe wasn't going well for Hitler, and you could tell this in the streets. The Germans, who had been happy to go to restaurants and the theater, were starting to crack down hard. Homes in which they found hidden weapons were often blown up. Everyone knew a story about someone getting into trouble. It scared me when Orlando came home and hid a Sten gun under his bed or a pistol in the center of a book. I knew that guns—and even parts to make bombs— went in and out of the house, but I wished I didn't. It wasn't that I didn't trust my brother: I didn't trust myself. I had started to became scared that I would tell someone something I wasn't supposed to by accident. I imagined myself being tortured by the Germans and giving away my whole family. The pressure of keeping my sister's secret was almost too much. I don't know why I had kept it so long, but the relief when I finally blurted it out was unbelievable.

One night, while Mama was performing, Papa came into my room to say goodnight. I hadn't heard him enter. I thought he was talking to Uncle Johann, so I was looking out into the yard to watch Masha and her young man. Papa's hand on my shoulder made me jump.

"What is it, Bamse?"

"Nothing . . . nothing." Suddenly, the secret was too much for me, and I turned and began sobbing into his jacket. "It's Masha, Papa, she has a German boyfriend—he's a soldier and she said if I tell she'll kill me, but I'm scared and I don't know what to do."

I could hardly breathe I was sobbing so hard, and Papa held me tight.

"My own sister," I cried.

"I know," he soothed, "I know." I could see the pain in his face. His daughter and his brother.

I looked at him, tears streaming down his kind face. "Papa, what if everything we are doing goes wrong?"

He held me by both arms and looked straight at me. "Bamse, my dear boy, good deeds can never be wrong—there are higher laws which must be obeyed. Stay here."

Papa left my room and I heard him go out into the yard. There was a commotion and I think someone got kicked by the cow. The next thing I knew, Papa, my thin Papa, was pulling this young man into the sitting room. Masha was crying, and the German soldier looked terrified. He sat curled up on the couch where Papa had thrown him, completely bewildered.

I had raced out of my bedroom at the noise and now stood in the doorway, wondering if I should look for one of Orlando's guns.

"What the hell do you think you are doing?" Papa yelled at my sister. "Do you want to get us all killed?"

"I won't hurt you," murmured the soldier. He couldn't have been more than seventeen. Younger than Orlando. To be honest, he didn't look as if he could hurt anyone even if he wanted to. He too had begun to cry. He certainly didn't look like a member of some master race.

"Papa, this is Boris," said Masha quietly.

He had a name. I don't know why, but suddenly he seemed more human. I didn't want to feel like this. We had an enemy in the house, and I should have been ready to kill him. Papa seemed to have collapsed a little, and I didn't think he would kill him either. Not on Mama's good carpet anyway.

I don't know what Papa would have done next if the front door hadn't banged open and Mama burst into the house with Thomas. She was screaming. Thomas was screaming. You couldn't tell who was the most upset. Papa and I leaped out into the hall and he grabbed her and tried to make her sit down.

"What is it, Marie? What's happened?"

"Orlando!" she screamed. "Orlando . . ." For once she didn't quote from anything. She just looked at Papa and said, "Orlando has been arrested. They say he will go to a labor camp." And with that she fainted dead away in Papa's arms.

"Marie!" yelled Papa, cradling her in a complete daze. Thomas was beside himself, and Masha just kept crying and saying how sorry she was. Boris leaped to his feet and picked up Mama in his arms, just as my brother would have done if he had been there. He motioned to me to show him where to put her, and I led him to her bedroom. The young private was very gentle with her. He placed her carefully on the bed, helping Thomas to arrange the cushions to protect her head. Papa followed and sat in the small chair by her makeup table. He didn't speak.

As if all this were not enough, Uncle Johann chose that moment to return. He came upon this rather tense scene and beamed when he saw the soldier.

"Heil Hitler!" he declared, and shot up his arm in a Nazi salute, but Boris said nothing. He looked at Masha, kissed her gently on the cheek, and I think he whispered good-bye. Then he moved to stand in front of my father. They looked at each other. There was a terrible silence, and then Boris gave a small bow of respect and left. Papa never moved. We all looked at Mama lying on the bed. It was such a pity she was unconscious. She would have loved the drama of it all.

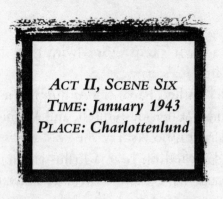

ACT II, SCENE SIX
TIME: *January 1943*
PLACE: *Charlottenlund*

<u>*None of the mothers*</u> dealt very well with
Orlando being taken. I burst into Anton's flat to tell
him, and Mrs. B. fainted on the spot before I had said
a word. The women were going down like pins in a
bowling alley. Once we had got her up again, Anton
and I had a conference on the balcony.

"What has he been arrested for?" whispered
Anton. I hadn't thought about it, but I suppose he was
worried that it might have been for something we had
taken part in. I didn't know who to be most worried
for—my mother, father, Orlando, Anton, his parents,
or even myself. If they could take my brilliant brother,
then we might well be next. I felt ashamed to be
thinking about myself.

"Maybe it's that law that bans all communist
organizations."

Anton frowned. "But Orlando isn't a communist."

"No, but he's certainly done enough in the resistance for the Germans to want him out of the way."

"But how do they know that? Orlando has been
so careful. I wonder what else they know?" Anton

crossed his arms and frowned. "Where have they taken him?"

"I don't know. They grabbed him in the street but I have no idea where he is now, and I don't suppose anyone will tell us."

Without Orlando to lead the way, it was difficult to know what to do. After that night Masha stayed home with Mama. I don't think she ever saw her soldier again. Papa could hardly bring himself to speak to her, and she crept about the apartment like an animal with an injured paw. Thomas also refused to leave and slept like a cat at the foot of Mama's bed while she cried in her sleep for her eldest son. Papa had tried to find out where my brother had been taken, but you couldn't ask too many questions as that might make things worse. It was awful.

I think even Uncle Johann was shocked.

"But why, Peter?" he asked Papa. "Orlando is just a boy."

"I know that, Johann—they are all just boys trying to fight these invaders you seem to think so highly of. Well done, brother, now your blessed troops have taken my son."

"Maybe you shouldn't have let him get involved in the resistance," declared Uncle Johann defensively.

I could hear Papa take a deep breath. "Maybe, Johann, he didn't think he had a choice when even his own uncle won't stand up for his country."

"I am standing up for my country. If we don't cooperate, you know that the French or the English will attack."

"Johann, that is nonsense. It is German propaganda. The Germans are not invincible. They are not protecting us from the French or the English. Stop being so afraid. We can beat this."

"I am not afraid, I just . . . I don't know anymore."

Johann's voice faltered; then he swept out of the apartment, almost crying. He ran down past Anton and me, sitting on the stairs. My uncle's footsteps echoed on the stone steps as we sat listening to Mama's sobbing. Upstairs, Mrs. B. was also crying softly, and we couldn't bear to be in either apartment. For a long time we didn't say anything at all, then Anton said, "What about the perforating machines?"

"The what?"

Anton lowered his voice to a whisper. "The perforators . . . you know . . . the guns Orlando had. Where are they?"

I shrugged. Orlando hadn't told me everything. "In his room somewhere, I guess."

Anton nodded. "Well, the first thing we need to do is get those to the rifle club."

I looked at Anton in disbelief. "Anton, we can't do that. You don't understand. Orlando didn't tell me everything. I don't know how to find the rifle club. I don't know who is in charge."

Anton looked at me with his big dark eyes. "Then we have to find out. We'll go to the paper. Someone there will tell us what to do."

I was terrified. Without my brother there I didn't want anything to do with the resistance. "We can't. The guns are dangerous and—"

Anton put his hand on my shoulder. "Bamse, I know you are afraid, but this isn't just about us. We can't give up now."

"I don't know, Anton. Maybe we should ask Papa."

Anton shook his head. "No. He will have enough to worry about. Come on, we can do this." He put his small shoulders back and headed for the door.

For some time now I had been feeling inclined not to do anything. I grabbed his arm. "I don't know, Anton, maybe it's too soon. Maybe they'll be watching us. Don't you think we should lie low for a bit?"

Anton turned and looked at me. "It's all right for you to give up, Bamse, you're not Jewish, but I don't have a choice. If they've taken Orlando, then we could be next. You stay if you want, but I have to do this for my family."

It was the only time we mentioned the difference between us. I felt ashamed of myself. Anton turned to go, and quietly I followed after him.

The streets seemed quieter, more menacing. We parked our bikes around the corner and headed to the dentist's office. There had been a password to get in but now there was no need. The door was hanging off its hinges and the place was deserted. There were papers and pieces of smashed equipment all over the floor.

Anton stood in the middle of the mess and shook his head. "Someone's given the location away."

"But who?" I couldn't imagine any of the people we had met doing such a thing. Outside, we could hear a truck passing by. I wanted to run away as fast as possible. Being at the paper had been great when the presses were whirring and the secret news was being printed, but now I felt as though there were Germans hiding behind every door. Who was it in that room with us who had given Orlando away?

"What do we do now, Anton?" I asked. "We don't know who we can trust."

Anton looked at me and held out his hand. "We can trust each other, Bamse," he said, and we solemnly shook on our friendship. I knew from the look in Anton's eye that he wouldn't let me give in, but I also knew it was going to mean trouble.

ACT II, SCENE SEVEN
TIME: *January 1943*
PLACE: *Copenhagen*

From the time Orlando was arrested, Papa was mostly out, but he didn't tell us where. He said the less we knew, the better, and I suppose we thought the same about him. Uncle Johann came back late at night and left early, so we didn't see him much either. As soon as we returned from the dentist's, Anton and I stole down the corridor to Orlando's room. I followed him with a heavy heart. Having a daring friend was becoming quite exhausting. We searched Orlando's room and managed to find three guns and some bullets hidden in various places.

Anton pulled a small metal box from under the bed and opened it. He gave a sharp intake of breath and sat down on the floor.

"What is it?" I asked.

"I'm not sure, but I think it's bomb parts."

"Sssh." I looked around, terrified that someone might hear; that Uncle Johann might be in the corridor. It was as though we had discovered treasure. We sat and stared at the wires and timers in the box. There were no instructions and neither one of us was quite sure how to put the bits together. We both had several Boy Scout badges, but none of them had covered explosives. We put the box back, but I knew that wouldn't be the end of it. I knew Anton wouldn't be able to resist.

The guns turned out to be easy to get rid of. We overheard Papa talking to a friend about a place in the park where the rifle club sometimes left things. One evening we went down there and left the pistols wrapped in a blanket. We weren't sure it was the right thing to do, but it seemed better than leaving them under Orlando's bed. It was on the way back that Anton hatched his plan.

"This is no good, you know, Bamse."

"What?"

"We can't just stop being active because Orlando isn't here to give us instructions. We should do something."

"Like what?" I asked apprehensively.

Anton shrugged. "I don't know. Some action, some sabotage or something. Just think how pleased Orlando would be if we managed to blow something up."

It was a thought that had never crossed my mind. Anton and I had become brilliant at taping things to the undersides of railway carriages and passing on bits of paper, but this was quite a bit more dramatic. Within a couple of days, Anton had decided that we should blow up a railway bridge.

Sabotage is not as easy as you might think. There was a best-selling book at the time—a sort of cookbook with recipes for homemade explosives and grenades—but neither of us knew how to get hold of it. Doing our best to remember what we had learned in physics at school, and with the assistance of some surprisingly helpful books from the library, we made what we believed to be two fine and deadly bombs. Our two "saboteur specials"—or "Norwegian noisemakers," as Anton called them—were quite different from each other because we didn't have more than one of any of the components. One was supposed to be what the books called an incendiary device—something that would cause a fire—and the other was just supposed to cause a great big explosion.

Having put so many papers under the trains at Hovedbanegården, we knew quite a lot about when the freight left and where it was going. We decided to set off our bombs on the night we knew the Germans would be sending the boat train to Sweden. We both agreed that we didn't want to kill anyone—not unless things got very desperate—so we planned for the bombs to go off on a bridge just before the train arrived.

When the big night of industrial sabotage arrived, it was pouring with rain, and I thought maybe that would mean we could put the whole thing off for another day, but Anton turned up at the front door grinning with excitement. "Isn't the weather perfect?" he said. "No one will be out to see what we are up to."

The rain was falling from the sky in great sheets. The crashing weather plus all the blackout restrictions meant that it was too dark to see your hand in front of your face. Neither Anton nor I liked the dark, but we were saboteurs now and there had to be some sacrifices. We both had trouble slipping out of the house because our mothers slept so lightly, but at last we met down in the yard, carrying our homemade devices under our jackets.

"They're getting wet," I moaned.

"That'll be all right," Anton said, ever the optimist. "Once the fire starts they'll dry out."

I couldn't imagine a fire at all in this weather, but I didn't like to say so. Hardly able to see where we were going, we two saviors of Denmark headed off on our bikes to the bridge. It was only when we got there that we realized there were a few things we hadn't thought of. We stood, soaked to the skin, and looked at the bridge.

"It's made of iron," said Anton.

"That won't burn, will it?" I replied.

He shook his head like a dog after a bath, so that drops of water flew around him.

"Well, maybe the explosion will still work. Maybe it will make a hole big enough to stop the train."

We stood for another moment, still looking at the heavy metal construction. Anton cleared his throat.

"Bamse, where do you suppose one puts a bomb on a bridge?"

We weren't sure. In the end we decided to put the thing in the middle, but even that wasn't easy. In the rain none of the tape we had brought would stick to the bridge, and Anton was beginning to get worried about his mother waking up. At last we wedged the thing in a crossbar and lit the fuse. It went out. We lit it again. It went out again.

"We'll have to stand here while it catches," said Anton.

So we did. We stood and sheltered the fuse while it burned down. It was only in the last seconds that I realized how incredibly stupid this was.

"Anton, run!"

Our sports master at school would have been proud of us. I don't think either of us had ever shown that kind of speed before. We leaped from the bridge and threw ourselves down a dirt bank by the side of the tracks. Our breathing was hard and painful and I desperately wanted to pee. Then—silence.

"I don't think it's worked," whispered Anton.

"No," I confirmed, and looked up from where I was lying. At that moment I should have remembered my father's advice about never going back to a firework once you have lit it. Anton and I had just stepped onto the bridge when the explosion happened. It was very loud. There was a lot of smoke. When it cleared, Anton and I were lying on the bridge, and even in the rain I knew that I had definitely wet myself. The bridge, however, was unmoved. We slowly inched over to the crossbar where the bomb had been. A hole about the size of a one-kroner coin had been blown in a small metal plate. Otherwise there was no damage at all.

In the distance I could see the twisted gold and copper spire of the Church of Our Saviour at Christianshavn, the island between Copenhagen and Amager, where Sallie Besiakov had her hat shop. I remembered what Papa had said about the man throwing himself from the tower. I didn't know if it was true, but I thought about Sallie's grandfather and his Cossack hats and about Papa saying you should do the best you could at everything, and I felt pretty low.

Anton and I cycled home in silence: hopeless saboteurs possibly in trouble with their mothers for being out in the cold. I would have done anything to have Orlando with us.

ACT II, SCENE EIGHT
TIME: *April 1943*
PLACE: *Charlottenlund*

It was the spring of 1943 when Papa came home with news. Uncle Johann had been staying for some time now and he was sitting in the kitchen. The two brothers hardly spoke anymore, and being in the same room with them was very uncomfortable.

Papa sat down. He looked exhausted. "A Danish woman has been shot on Knippel Bridge."

Uncle Johann gave a sort of snort. "What had she done?"

Papa looked at him. "Nothing, Johann. She had done nothing. As far as anyone knows, she wasn't even a member of the resistance. Just a woman out minding her own business, walking home quietly and peacefully with some shopping when a bored German soldier took aim and shot her down. She died shortly after being admitted to Sunby Hospital. Happy now?"

Johann looked shocked. "I didn't kill her."

Papa stood up and said quietly, "You might as well have done." He went to see Mama in her room, and I remember Uncle Johann just sitting there, not saying a word.

Things were getting more and more tense. Not just in our house but in the streets as well.

A regiment of Danish Nazis who had fought with Germans on the eastern front returned to Copenhagen. A large group of them had gathered in Radhuspladsen, the town hall square, to celebrate. I was on my way past to deliver something for the paper, which was up and running again. I stopped to look. I wanted to see what Danes who wouldn't defend their country looked like. There were German posters everywhere showing blond Danes apparently shaking hands with German soldiers in the fight *mot Bolsjevismen*—against bolshevism. They claimed that we were all facing a common enemy. There were some people who believed it, but it was hard to tell who they were and I wanted to see for myself. I wasn't the only one. Pretty soon there was quite a crowd around them. Then a woman called out, "Traitors!"

Soon others were beginning to chant things and shout at the young Nazis. I knew there was going to be trouble. I looked across the mob and standing on the edge, I saw Uncle Johann. He looked old and tired and even a little confused. He didn't seem to be on either side in the arguments, which were growing louder by the minute. He looked at me and moved as if to say something, but just then someone threw a punch. I don't know which side it came from, but in seconds there was fighting all around me and I cycled like mad to get away. That night, for the first time, there was rioting in the street. Hitler's Canary had had enough and wanted out of the cage.

Mama had started back at the theater, but Thomas still stayed with us every night. When she wasn't working, Mama wore just black all the time. She never dressed up anymore and the spark seemed to have gone out of her. Uncle Johann didn't come back that night, and no one knew where he had gone. Although the atmosphere was better in the house, I know it made Papa very unhappy. Masha didn't see Boris anymore, but many nights I saw her standing in the yard with Mrs. Jensen's cow, Bess, crying and looking out into the street behind. It was a sad time for everyone, but there was worse to come.

One night Papa and I were sitting in the conservatory together. He looked exhausted. We hadn't heard a word about Orlando for some time. He lowered his voice to a whisper.

"Bamse, I heard some news today." Papa stopped and looked at me. Suddenly I realized that he had stopped treating me like his little boy; that we were fighting together and that he trusted me. "Orlando has been transferred from prison to Bispebjerg Hospital with some kind of stomach trouble."

"Who told you?" I asked.

"Your Uncle Johann."

"And you believe him?"

"I don't know. He seemed to be trying to help, but it is so hard to know who to trust and who is working on which side. I want to believe him. He is my brother but I don't know. . . ."

We sat together and thought about Orlando. What did it mean? Was he really ill or was it a ploy to get him out of the prison? Did this mean he might escape, or had the Germans treated him so badly that now he was ill? It was impossible to know.

The next day, after school, I was carrying a message in my shoe across the road at Store Kongensgade to a new drop for the paper, when someone came up behind me and whispered in my ear, "Bring clothes for your brother to Bispebjerg Hospital tomorrow. Tell no one."

It sounded like Uncle Johann but when I turned around to see who had spoken, the person had disappeared into the crowd. I didn't know what it meant; whether it was good news or not. Did telling no one include Anton and Papa? What kind of clothes did he need?

The next day I packed a bag with a few of my brother's things. I didn't know where he was going or what it was for, so I chose warm things. I put them in a shopping bag because I thought a suitcase might draw attention to me and cycled to the hospital. When I got there I wasn't sure what to do.

The woman behind the desk smiled at me. "Can I help you?"

"I . . . I'm looking for . . ."

"It's alright," she said. "You are safe here." And I believed her. Sometimes you just had to trust somebody. I took a deep breath and said, "I'm looking for Orlando Skovlund."

She nodded and looked up his name on her list. "Upstairs. Third bed on the right."

There he was, sitting up in bed and smiling at me. He looked thin and he had a slight beard, which made him look old, but I ran to him and he hugged and hugged me.

"Oh Bamse, my brave fighter."

"Oh Orlando, we miss you. Mama cries all the time and Anton and I tried to blow up a bridge and—"

Orlando laughed and told me to shush. "You are a good Norwegian worker." Then he held me close and whispered in my ear, "You must go now, Bamse. I'll see you soon. Tell Mama and Papa that I am fine. Go now."

A man was standing near Orlando's bed waiting to speak to him, and I knew it was time to leave. I could hardly see for tears but I knew my brother would want me to be brave, so I tried to walk tall and straight. I meant to ride straight home, but there was a small newsstand across from the hospital and I couldn't resist hiding behind it for a while to see if anything happened. It wasn't long before a car drew up at a side entrance and I saw Orlando come out and get in. He drove off in the clothes I had brought and somehow I knew it was OK. Mama cried when I told her, Papa nodded quietly, and we just carried on as if everyone were half asleep.

**The night after** Orlando escaped, Uncle Johann didn't come home. It would be some months before we saw him again, but we had other things to worry about. In March of 1943 a new Danish government had been elected, but there was no question anymore about who was really in charge. By July it had become a crime to even annoy the Germans, and they were really easy to annoy. You could get thirty days in prison for speaking English to a German soldier and the same for writing *Victoire* ("Victory" in French) on a German signboard. It seemed even the little stuff was beginning to get to our occupiers. We heard more and more stories about sabotage taking place. Attacks on railway lines and bridges, rather more successful than Anton's and mine, had become commonplace. Sometimes British RAF planes on bombing raids to Danish factories crash-landed and resistance groups helped to smuggle the downed officers to Sweden. Anton dreamed of finding a British pilot, and we were always on the lookout.

"Come with me. I am your friend," Anton would practice in careful English, but we never found one.

By August there must have been six or seven acts of sabotage every day in towns right across the country. In the town of Odense on the island of Fyn, a huge new German warship was blown up, and soon the Danish Nazi sympathizers, Uncle Johann's old crowd the Schalburg Corps, were out on the streets frightening everyone. The people had had enough and started to go on strike. The Germans imposed curfews and protestors gathered in the street. Soon things turned violent and the Germans often opened fire on the crowds.

For a week Anton and I were forbidden to leave home. Papa would come back every day with news no one wanted to hear.

"Torvald, the comic, is dead."

That funny man of the theater who had teased the German high command had been at the barricades, demanding that the Schalburg Corps withdraw from the city. How could he be dead? He had never tried to hurt anybody.

"I spoke to one of the doctors at Sunby Hospital," said Papa. "Six hundred and sixty-four Danes wounded so far, and eighty-seven killed in the rioting. There are bonfires and barricades everywhere but it is hopeless. The Germans are too strong."

However strong the Germans were, it didn't stop the resistance. The secret workers started getting more and more daring, and one night, August 24, 1943, we were woken up by the most massive explosion.

Papa ran to the window. We thought maybe the British had come, but we couldn't see troops anywhere. It wasn't till the next morning that we found out it was the Forum. Just northwest of Copenhagen in the town of Fredricksberg, the Forum, Denmark's largest exhibition hall, was being converted into a giant German barracks. At lunchtime on the day before it was due to open, a young delivery boy with what looked like a case of Tuborg beer on his bicycle went in the rear entrance to the Forum. Of course, he wasn't carrying beer at all but fifty kilos of explosives. Unlike Anton and me, this guy knew what he was doing. Only the steel skeleton of the building was left. I didn't know who the delivery boy was, but I hoped it was Orlando.

August 29 was my thirteenth birthday. Papa had painted me a picture of Mama to hang in my room. It was Mama before the war, sitting smiling on a balcony on holiday. It was how I remembered her, and it made me feel better. Mama had two kroner for me to buy sweets, and Thomas had sewn me a fine new jacket with a tiny teddy bear embroidered on the inside breast pocket.

"A bamse for a Bamse," he said, and kissed me on the forehead. He was a good man and Mama could not have managed without him.

That day Papa came home with the news. "The government has resigned. They were told to sign an agreement to stop all strikes and public gatherings and they wouldn't. Now we must be careful. All acts of sabotage, even the possession of a gun, are immediately punishable by death." We sat and listened to the announcement by the German General von Hanneken on the radio:

"Recent events have shown that the Danish government is no longer able to maintain peace and order in Denmark. The disturbances provoked by hostile agents are aimed directly at the Wehrmacht. Therefore . . . I declare a military state of emergency in the whole of Denmark."

Papa chewed on his pipe while Thomas sat at Mama's feet, helping her wind some wool. The room was lit only by the dim light from the glass panel on the radio. Masha brought in coffee and sat on the sofa with me. Papa turned off the radio and there was silence.

"I saw Boris today," said Masha. "I saw him drive by, sitting at attention in the back of a canvas-covered truck. He looked scared."

It was the first time Boris's name had been mentioned. Papa reached out and patted Masha's hand.

"He has reason to be. We all do. The king has placed himself under house arrest in Amalienborg Palace. Not that he could have got out anyway—but at least he is in the middle of things with the rest of us. The palace is surrounded by green ones."

"Who was taken today? Anyone we know?" asked Mama.

"Lots of Danes, Jewish or not. All the main officers of the Danish army, navy, and air force. They say that before he was taken, the rear admiral of the navy just had time to send a message to his men which simply ordered them to 'scuttle or escape to Sweden.' Twenty-nine ships were sunk, thirteen got to Sweden, and only six were captured by the Germans."

"Some pet canary for Hitler, eh?" sniffed Thomas.

Papa nodded. "I think even people who thought we could opt for peace and quiet know that there can be no more collaboration."

"And Uncle Johann?" I whispered, but no one answered.

It did seem as if the people of Denmark had collectively decided that we were not having Danes of any kind being treated badly. More and more citizens began protesting, and life became increasingly difficult. The Gestapo came in their green open trucks with canvas roofs—prairie wagons, we called them— and filled them with Danes who would never be seen again. I saw one truck stop outside the big clothing shop Knud Nielsen and Co. and take people from the flat above. All around people watched, but there was nothing anyone could do.

"Countrymen, hold your heads up," someone called from the crowd. Maybe it was a communist calling to a Jew. It didn't matter. It was terrible whoever you were. We were all in it together, and no one knew who would be next.

ACT II, SCENE TEN
TIME: *September 1943*
PLACE: *Copenhagen*

<u>*I was at home*</u> when Mr. Goldberger, the cantor from the synagogue, came to our flat. He lived across the way and I had often seen him to nod good morning as he passed on his way to work.

"Bamse, is your father home?"

"No," I replied. "Do you want to wait?"

Thomas came out of Mother's room with her teacup. He and Mr. Goldberger greeted each other like old friends.

Mr. Goldberger was shaking. "Thomas . . . the Gestapo . . . they have taken the librarian from the synagogue. I was at prayers when they just stormed in and took him away. Now they will be able to check the lists of our members. Every Jew in Copenhagen will be known to them. You, me, everyone."

It was like a light going on in my head. Thomas was part of the synagogue community. I had known him since I was a baby. It had never occurred to me that he might be on a list. He was just Thomas. How could he harm anyone?

"Thomas? You never said . . . ," I managed.

"My dear boy"—he smiled, stroking my face—"why should I? This is my country. I have no quarrel with anyone. I've never even spoken to a German."

Mr. Goldberger was getting agitated. "We must protect the papers from the synagogue, but when I try to warn the congregation, they say I am causing panic. I tell them about other Jews and the death camps, but no one wants to listen."

"I could phone Father," I offered. "He's at the office."

Thomas put his hand on the phone to stop me. "No. Too dangerous. Hurry. Go and tell the priest at Trinitatas Church, Pastor Madsen, to get ready. He'll understand. We will follow as quickly as we can."

"I'll get Anton."

Thomas grabbed both my arms and looked at me sternly. "No, Bamse. You must do this on your own. You need to be brave now. Anton cannot help you anymore. It is too dangerous for him."

I cycled for all I was worth to fetch the priest from the Trinity Church. My head was spinning. How could anything be too dangerous for my daring friend? He was so much braver than me.

It was a long way to the old Latin Quarter in the heart of the city but I knew it well. Mama thought Trinity was the most dramatic of the churches, with its high white walls and amazing gold chandeliers. She had often taken me there as a small child, and after the service we would climb the long, wide spiral stairway to the top of the wonderful round tower beside it. She would tell the story of how in 1716 the Empress Katharina had driven up to the top of the tower in a carriage, with her husband Peter the Great leading the way on horseback, to enjoy the beautiful view over Copenhagen.

Now no one had time for a beautiful view. The pastor seemed to be expecting me. He threw on his coat and together we raced to the synagogue. Thomas and Mr. Goldberger were already there. I had never been in a synagogue. It had always seemed a mysterious place to me, but actually it wasn't all that different from the church. It too was decorated in white and gold—rather simple, with light flooding into a central place called the Ark, where Mr. Goldberger and Thomas were hard at work.

The priest and the cantor clasped each other, and for a moment they knelt and each spoke to God in their own way. It was strange to me. It sounded so personal—as if God himself were in the room. Then they rose and began to pack the ten Torah scrolls with the Mosaic law, handwritten in Hebrew on parchment; the prayer shawls that Jews wear over their shoulders in the synagogue; prayer books; and other things. All these we took silently and hid them in the underground crypt below Pastor Madsen's church.

When it was done Thomas and I went back to the synagogue for one last look. We sat at the back and looked at the inscription in Hebrew above the Ark.

"What does it say, Thomas?" I asked.

"It says, 'Hear, O Israel, the Lord is our God, the Lord is One.' It is a declaration of faith," Thomas sighed. "We shall need it."

When I got back I raced up to Anton's apartment. Normally the door was unlocked and I would just go in, but as I reached it I realized that for the first time in my life, it was locked. I raised my hand to knock but I didn't want to frighten Mrs. B. I stood there not knowing what to do . . .

That night Papa was sitting with Thomas, discussing what might happen next. It was late and Papa was dressed for bed.

I had fallen asleep on the sofa and was woken up by a great thumping in the hall. I could vaguely hear Papa saying, "Thomas, you will have to go if the Germans decide to move the Jews."

Thomas was refusing: "I cannot leave Marie. She needs me."

Then Masha ran in and looked out of the window. "Soldiers, Papa, on the stairs."

Thomas's hand flew to his mouth to cover a gasp. Now the enemy were not just in our city, they were in our home. They passed by our door and on up to the Beilins' apartment. There was a wood-splintering bang on their door with what sounded like the butt of a rifle. Mama had taken a sleeping pill and seemed a little dazed, but the noise had awakened everyone. She leaned on Papa as he stood listening in his dressing gown and slippers. There seemed to be no answer from the Beilins. Masha reached out and took my hand. This was not a time to be horrid to anyone.

"Don't open your door, don't open your door," I whispered over and over again while I held my sister's hand.

Suddenly, Mama surprised us all by shouting out very loudly, "They've gone away! They're in the country! Stop that infernal noise or I shall call the police!"

Silence. The banging stopped. Perhaps they would come to us next. Perhaps they would take Thomas or me or Papa or Mama for shouting . . .

I don't think any of us drew a single breath. Then we heard the soldiers descending, getting into their truck, and driving away.

"Oh Marie, that was magnificent," breathed Papa.

Thomas wiped a tear from his eye. "She should go to Hollywood, you know, they don't have her like."

Mama raised her hand to acknowledge the praise. "Thank you, my dears. Entirely improvised, you know. The moment arrived and somehow I just knew what to say. They seem to be a people who like commands."

Thomas took Mama by the arm and led her back to her room as we all reflected that she was more marvelous than she had ever been.

It wasn't long before Anton was at the door.

"Papa's collapsed and Mama just sits on the bed, crying with Gilda. I don't know what to do."

He was frightened. More frightened than when the bomb went off.

"Bamse, Anton, fetch them down here now," commanded Papa. "They shall stay with us. Masha, wake Lisa and tell her to make some sandwiches and fresh coffee. It's going to be a long night."

Four nights later, on September 29—the Wednesday before Rosh Hashanah, the Jewish New Year—Rabbi Marcus Melchior could be seen on his bike, wearing a gray suit and carrying a brown paper parcel. He looked like any other Dane going about his business, which, of course, he was. That Wednesday morning there were perhaps eighty people in the Krystal Street synagogue for morning prayers, but the rabbi wasn't wearing his usual robe for services. Instead he stood up and said, "I have very important news to tell you. Last night I received word that the Germans plan to raid Jewish homes throughout Copenhagen to arrest all the Danish Jews for shipment to concentration camps. They know that tomorrow is Rosh Hashanah, so our families will be home. The situation is very serious. We must take action immediately. You must leave the synagogue now and contact all relatives, friends, and neighbors you know are Jewish and tell them what I have told you. You must speak to all your Christian friends and tell them to warn the Jews. You must do this immediately, within the next few minutes, so that two or three hours from now everyone will know what is happening. By nightfall tonight we must all be in hiding."

They say the news was leaked by a top German who didn't want to carry out Hitler's order. Whoever it was, everyone told everyone else the news. Papa had heard from a local contact at the Social Democratic Party, and he sent me out to warn anyone I could think of.

"You must go up every street, find anyone with a Jewish name, and tell them to go into hiding now. They must not wait. The Germans are sure that all the Jews will be at home for Rosh Hashanah. There is very little time."

"Anton can't come, can he?" I asked.

Papa stroked my face. "No, Bamse. You must go alone. It is not safe for Anton. He must hide too. Tell everyone to leave now and go to the nearest hospital. The doctors and nurses will hide them until we can get them away from the city."

Masha came in from the hall. She was wearing her coat. "He doesn't have to go alone, Papa. I'll go with you, Bamse," she said. Papa looked at Masha and frowned.

"I'm on your side, Papa. Liking Boris didn't mean I was a traitor. You didn't know him. He's just as scared as the rest of us."

Papa pulled her to him and then he hugged us both. "Be safe, my babies. Go now."

Nothing was safe for Anton anymore. Nothing was safe for anyone. Masha and I cycled up every street we could think of. Skt. Pedersstræde, Vestergade, Studiestræde—anywhere—looking for Jewish names on doorbells and telling the inhabitants what was happening. I wasn't always sure what a Jewish name was, so sometimes I just rang the bell and told the people to warn their friends.

"Where shall we go? What shall we do?" the frightened families asked.

"Go to the hospital. You'll be safe there," I assured them, hoping it was true. Once they were on their way, I would remove their nameplate, and Masha, who had the best handwriting, would write *Jensen* under the doorbell instead. Suddenly the city was full of people called Jensen. Some went to the hospital; some knew my father and wanted to speak to him first. They followed us home, and soon we were gathering Jewish families like small boys bring home abandoned puppies.

The worst was when people didn't believe us. One family—the Abrahamovitzes—were just about to have their evening meal when Masha and I called. We were both tired now and felt as though we had said the same thing over and over a thousand times. There were five of them all gathered together, saying Hebrew prayers.

"Shalom aleichem," I began in Hebrew to show I was on their side. Mrs. B. had taught me and I thought it would help. "You must hurry. I have come to tell you to flee. Go now to the Bispebjerg Hospital and the doctors will help get you to Sweden. Just take a small bag and some flowers to look like you are visiting someone. No suitcases. Leave everything behind."

The family sat silently, looking first at me and then at Masha.

"Please," Masha pleaded. "We've been sent by the Social Democratic Party to bring this message. You must go now. There isn't time to discuss it."

"This is ridiculous," said the father, standing up. "I won't believe it."

"Please, sir, it's true."

"You are lying," he insisted. "We have been told that we are safe, that no one will be taken. There will be no persecution of the Jews."

"It's not true. They are coming." I was almost choking as I tried to persuade this man I had never met before to leave his home and run.

"Well, I shall ring the chief rabbi and ask him."

"No!" I yelled. "You mustn't use the phones. You must leave or . . . or . . . I will . . ."

I stopped as I couldn't think of anything to threaten them with. I didn't want to threaten them. They were in enough trouble already. Exhausted and frightened, I burst into tears. Masha put her arms around me and she too began to cry. It was all too much. Now the mother stood up and laid her hand on her husband's arm.

"Solomon, why would the children come if it were not true? Come, we have no one else to trust."

Over the next couple of days, people came and went in the flat and more and more arrived to stay. Some people were philosophical: "In my family relatives all over the world—people always fleeing. Not a member of my family who hasn't helped support the suitcase maker."

Others were still with shock and terror. Terrors from the past and terrors from the present. Anton's father, Mr. Beilin, sat in a corner and never moved. He seemed almost dead while all around him was endless activity. Papa would get a message saying so and so had six kilos of potatoes for him, and of course that meant six people, and Papa would arrange for the "delivery." The Goldbergers came, the Beilins from upstairs, Sallie Besiakov and two of her staff, Mr. Kaufmann from the theater and his wife, and several others whom I didn't know at all. People I recognized from the newspaper printing came and went with hushed words:

"Ritzau's news bureau has been occupied to stop anyone using the telex for information."

"There are convoys of German trucks driving up and down Strøget and Købmager Street."

Mama, Masha, and Lisa cooked and cooked and everyone tried to keep the little ones amused as they couldn't go outside. Thomas made dressing–up clothes for the kids, and for Gilda, Anton's sister, a special teddy bear with a pink bow around its neck to match her dress.

The night of Friday, October 1, Papa sat and talked to the men.

"We can't go anywhere, Peter," one of them declared. "All exit roads to the city are now occupied by German soldiers. They are stopping and searching everyone."

Papa tried to piece it all together. "We hear that the Nazi plan was for a lightning attack today and tomorrow. They want to round up all Danish Jews as quickly as possible."

"And then?" asked the cantor.

Papa took a deep breath and lowered his voice so that the children couldn't hear. "You are to be transported to the Theresienstadt concentration camp in Czechoslovakia."

"But it is the Sabbath. It is Rosh Hashanah," wailed Mr. Kaufmann.

Papa nodded. "That's why they thought everyone would be at home. The phone lines have already been disconnected."

Mr. Goldberger shook his head. "I thought everyone said they would never do this. We are Danes."

A friend of Orlando's from the rifle club arrived and gave Papa a package. No one said what it was but I knew it was a gun.

"How are things in the street?" everyone asked.

The young man looked pale. "The troops are angry. They can't find anyone to arrest."

Within three days almost every Jew in the country had gone into hiding. A small halfhearted cheer went up and Mama shushed everyone. Our messenger paused. "Stuck for people to arrest, they've taken all the residents at the Jewish old people's home in Krystal Street. They say the German police troops went to the synagogue to take what was left and relieved themselves in the building."

"How can this be happening?" wept Mrs. B. over and over again while Anton stood helplessly patting her shoulder. "How can this be happening?"

Anton looked at me and I didn't have an answer. I didn't know what to say to him. The truth is that no one had known this was going to happen. There had been talk, but most people believed Denmark was too important to the Germans for any of the people to be deported. Now something had to be done, but it was like Mama that night they banged on the Beilins' door—the plan was entirely improvised.

Papa got busy trying to sort out contacts to get our newly enlarged family of friends to Sweden, where they would be safe.

That Sunday, October 3, a statement from Bishop Fuglsang-Damgaard was read in all the Lutheran churches of Denmark, reminding everyone that Jesus had been born a Jew. From every pulpit the Danes were told:

We understand by freedom of religion the right to exercise our faith in God in such a way that race and religion can never in themselves be reason for depriving a man of his rights, freedom, or property. Despite different religious views, we shall therefore struggle to ensure the continued guarantee to our Jewish brothers and sisters of the same freedom we ourselves treasure more than life itself.

Martial law was declared: No gathering of more than five people permitted . . . Curfew at nightfall . . . No mail, telephone, or telegraph service until further notice . . . All strikes prohibited and punishable by death . . . All offenses to be punished by German military courts.

It would have been very scary and I suppose it was, but over the next few days we had work to do.

"Marie, what was the name of that fisherman in Sletten who was such a fan of yours?" Papa would call out, while Mama, for some reason, went into full *Macbeth* mode. She wore a long brocade gown with trailing sleeves and kept calling out at intervals:

"Hang out our banners on the outward walls;
The cry is still 'They come': our castle's strength
Will laugh a siege to scorn . . ."

I don't know if she was being brave or acting brave but it worked. Everyone thought she was magnificent. Slowly Papa was starting to organize contacts to get small groups out of the flat and on their way across the water. We tried to listen to the radio and quiet cheers went up when the Swedes broadcast that, contrary to their previous policy of not getting involved, they would now accept all Danish Jews who wished to come to their country.

All across Denmark in homes like ours, in inns, churches, warehouses, lofts, barns, and cellars, more than seven thousand people were hidden from the German authorities. The Germans announced:

> As a result of measures taken by the German authorities, the Jews have been removed from public life and prevented from continuing to poison the atmosphere, for it is they who have to a considerable degree been responsible for the deterioration of the situation in Denmark through anti-German incitement and moral and material support for acts of terror and sabotage.

No one believed a word. Well, nearly no one. Sadly, there were still those who were not on our side.

ACT III, SCENE TWO
TIME: October 1943
PLACE: Charlottenlund

<u>*Quite a few of our "guests"*</u> had come and gone when Masha got word that we were in trouble. She came in flushed and cold one evening. Lisa the cook hadn't been around all day, so Mama and Thomas were making pancakes for everyone. I had never seen Mama in the kitchen, and despite everything, she was laughing, with flour all over her face. It was lovely. Little Gilda Beilin wouldn't leave Thomas's side anymore, and he was flipping tiny pancakes in the air for her and her teddy. The Beilin family was still staying with us because Papa didn't think Mr. Beilin could be moved. He was quite gone in the head, and Anton's mother had developed a severe skin rash.

Papa came and went and brought back news or plans.

"Marie," he would call when he returned, and they would hug as if they hadn't seen each other for months. She would stroke his face as he recounted his adventures.

"You'll like this—some blasted stikker"—our name for an informer—"phoned the Danish police to say a group of Jews were about to escape. So, of course, the police do their duty and arrive with their paddy wagon. They arrest the Jews and drive them off under arrest. In fact, they drove them to Snekkersten on the northern coast, where they let them out and told them to look up the innkeeper at Snekkersten Kro, who would get them to Sweden."

Our next visitors were an elderly couple, a Mr. and Mrs. Isak, whom the rifle club had found hiding in Ørsted Park. They had been too frightened to trust anyone and had been faint with hunger by the time the university boys had persuaded them to trust us. The old woman was marvelous.

"If I hadn't been so angry at those Nazis," she declared, as Thomas passed her bread and salt, "I would have died a long time ago."

It was then that Masha came in with her news. "Mama," she said almost in a whisper, "Mama, we're in danger." And then she sat down at the kitchen table and wept.

"I . . . Boris says—"

"You were not to see him," admonished Papa, looking shaken. "I thought you had realized . . . that you were on our side—"

"I haven't, honest, Papa, I haven't." Masha looked at him with tears streaming down her face. "He sent a note. He says the SS are watching our flat, and we should expect a visit from them any time. Someone told on us. Boris was trying to help."

A shiver went around the room. Who? Who would do such a thing? We had heard quite a few stories about stikkers, who would tell the Germans what was going on. Everyone knew that Gestapo Juhl, a Danish-speaking man from southern Jutland, and his gang were operating in this area.

"My bastard brother," muttered Papa. It was the only time I ever heard him swear.

"Yes, well," said Mama, "we've no time for that. We have work to do. If they are going to come here, we need to be prepared."

"How?" moaned Thomas. "It is hours till dark and we can't possibly move everyone during the day."

"This is a flat," said Papa. "We don't have a loft or a cellar to hide anyone in."

"My dearest Thomas, my darling husband, relax. We will do what we do best—we will put on a show," declared Mama, and just as if she were in the theater, she took charge. She marched into the farthest of our reception rooms with her hands on her hips.

"Yes. A wall. About here. With the right lighting . . . Peter, you will build the set. Bamse, fetch your father's tools. Thomas, I shall need a different outfit." Soon we were all at work.

Papa had been making magic in the theater for years. Now he did it in our own flat. Just like a flat piece of scenery in the theater, he built a false wall out of a timber frame and two linen sheets stretched tight and nailed into place. Mr. Isak turned out to be a carpenter, and soon he and Papa had a solid frame that stood about a meter out from the real wall. This left a gap behind, where about half a dozen people could just about squeeze in. At first I couldn't imagine what use it could possibly be, but then Papa got to work with his brushes and painted the huge canvas to look exactly like the rest of the room.

Mama reappeared in her satin dressing gown and stood looking at his work. "Not bad," she muttered, "but it needs dressing. Thomas!"

Thomas emerged from her room carrying a large potted plant. "I know, Marie, I know. It needs help," he agreed.

Thomas and Mama went to work changing the lighting, placing a few potted plants on stands and a couple of easy chairs in front of the wall. I had seen this done a million times in the theater but never to such good effect. The painted sheets and wood were transformed into a rather dull sitting-room wall, where chairs and plants had come to rest quite naturally. Which was exactly what Mama wanted.

When she and Thomas were satisfied, Papa pulled the false wall back far enough to leave a small gap, and behind it we made a space for Mr. and Mrs. Beilin, Gilda, Anton, Thomas, and the elderly Isaks. Masha went to get a little food and water to put with them because we had no idea how long they would need to be there.

Anton stood looking at the wall with me. "I don't want to hide, Bamse," he said.

"I know."

"I'm not really afraid," he continued, and although his lip trembled, we both pretended that was true. We were both terrified.

"Thank you," he managed.

"Don't be silly, you idiot. You'd do the same for me."

"Come along, come along, you two. This is not Shakespeare. No need for big good-byes. Let's get moving," directed Mama. "Now I need a bed in . . . yes—the conservatory. That's about as far from the false wall as we can get and the light in here will distract them from looking into too many corners."

Anton and I laid out the bed in the conservatory, and while we were working he whispered to me, "Where's the gun?"

"What gun?"

"The one Orlando stole from the soldiers at La Tosca all that time ago."

"I don't know. He must have hidden it."

"Well, it's not in his room because we checked that."

Then I remembered. I scrabbled around in a few of the conservatory potted plants and there it was, hidden under a great red geranium. Orlando had wrapped it in some cloth. I shook the dirt from the covering and brought out the German pistol just as Mama came in to check on our work. She was dressed in what appeared to be a lace nightgown and carrying her makeup box from the theater.

"Where did you get that, Bamse?" she demanded.

"Orlando took it. From the soldiers at La Tosca."

"Throw it away," she ordered.

"But we might need it."

Papa came in and looked at her and then at me. "It's true, Marie, we might."

She gave a little shiver. "I don't like it. Remember what Chekhov said: 'If in Act One you have a pistol hanging on the wall, then it must fire in the last act.' That's all I'm saying." She swept back to her bedroom with Thomas.

I wasn't sure what it meant. I knew Papa already had a gun, and I was about to give him this one when there was a knock at the door. My heart banged in my chest as if it wanted to get out. Hardly able to breathe, I shoved the gun back into the flowerpot and dropped the geranium back down on top of it.

"Screw your courage to the sticking place!" yelled Mother from behind her door. Papa raced to get everyone in place. Anton, his family, and Mr. and Mrs. Isak were placed behind the false wall and everything put back to camouflage the secret space. As we pushed the wall into place, I realized we had forgotten Thomas.

"Papa," I called, but it was too late. He was opening the front door. If he had planned to act calm and controlled, then things didn't quite turn out as expected. Standing in the doorway was Uncle Johann. I think it was the tension of the moment, but without a single moment's hesitation, Papa pulled back his fist and slammed Uncle Johann right on the jaw.

ACT III, SCENE THREE
TIME: *October 1943*
PLACE: *Charlottenlund*

<u>**Uncle Johann reeled**</u> and then almost fell into the apartment—at which point Papa, my mild-mannered father, hit him again. Johann fell forward, cracking his head on the hall table where people usually left their gloves. Blood gushed from his temple onto the black-and-white tiled floor as he lay there groaning.

"Peter, Peter," he gasped, "I came to warn you. Lisa, the cook, has told the Gestapo about—" And with that, Uncle Johann passed out.

"Peter, what are you doing?" called Mama from her room.

"I think I've killed my brother," he replied.

"Excellent," came the icy response. "Well, better tuck him away as well before anyone else shows up. There's always a danger that drama may turn into farce," she muttered as she went about her preparations.

But Uncle Johann wasn't dead, not unless the dead do a lot of moaning.

"Masha, get some bandages!" yelled Papa.

"Why would we have bandages?" yelled back Masha, who, although she had never liked Uncle Johann, liked blood even less. In the end she found some cloths in the kitchen, which Papa wrapped around his brother's head. Then Papa and I dragged him over to the false wall.

"I'm sorry, Peter, I wanted to warn you. I wanted to help," mumbled Uncle Johann, almost delirious.

"I'm sorry, Johann, I'm so sorry," Papa kept repeating while his brother groaned. "I didn't know."

We had to move all the potted plants and chairs and everything to get him behind there, and by the time we had finished, we were both sweating like mad. Masha was trying to clean the blood off the tiles, but it kept smearing into the cracks because she was mostly doing it with her eyes shut.

Mama's door opened and she reappeared. She looked terrible. Her face was as pale as her nightdress and she had great dark circles under her eyes. She was helped by an elderly nurse who, although stooped and gray, seemed to have the strength to assist Mama. They stopped and eyed the rather pathetic attempts to clean up the blood.

"Put a rug over it," Thomas's voice came from the nurse. It was quite spooky. I looked again. Thomas was the nurse. It was brilliant but it was also weird. He made rather a good nurse. In fact, rather a better nurse than a man.

"Papa . . . ," I whispered.

"Not now," he replied, patting my arm.

"Come along, madam, time to rest," Thomas said in a high-pitched voice as he led Mama to the conservatory.

She looked feeble until she called with huge command over her shoulder, "Leave the front door open. I don't want them breaking the thing down."

Masha threw a rug down in the hall over Uncle Johann's blood and we all went to see how the invalid was doing. Mama was lying on the day bed in the conservatory but she wasn't happy.

"It won't do, Thomas. It would be fine for stage, but this is close-up work we're doing. Much more like film than theater. Bamse, get me a sharp kitchen knife, and Thomas, the makeup box."

We both scooted off. I gave Mama the vegetable knife. Without a moment's hesitation she pulled up her nightie to the top of her thighs and looked at her beautiful but pale legs.

"Ah, well," she sighed, and then she began to make long, single cuts across her legs with the sharp blade. I thought Papa was going to faint. He sat down in a small chair in the corner and didn't speak. Thomas seemed to know what she was doing, for he carefully mopped the blood and then began to apply makeup on and around the fresh wounds. It wasn't long before Mama's legs were so disfigured that any glance at them would suggest she might never walk again.

Across the way we could see torches flash in the Goldbergers' apartment and then the lights went on. The shadows of SS officers going about their searches were clearly visible. There was no more time. They would be with us in a moment. We sat and waited, Mama lying on the bed, Thomas beside her pretending to take her pulse, Papa mopping his forehead where the old burn across his face seemed to be glowing in the semidark, Masha trying to look at the plants, and me lying on the floor, seemingly absorbed in a book.

Not six meters from us the families lay hidden and silent beside a comatose Uncle Johann.

"Bamse!" Masha whispered urgently.

"What?"

"Your book! It's upside down."

**We sat like actors** in a play waiting for the appearance of the bad guy. It wasn't long before we heard their heavy tread on the front step. They didn't knock but entered and walked straight through to the conservatory. It was as if they knew the layout of the apartment exactly. There were five of them—four Danes from the Schalburg Corps and one German SS officer. They were big men with short, sharp haircuts. In their uniforms and carrying their guns they looked terrifying, but Papa managed to stand as they entered and gave a small nod.

"Good evening, gentlemen. You have come to call perhaps on the great Marie Skovlund. We have had many visitors in her last days. You are welcome."

The men had searched many apartments that evening, but this was the first time anyone had said they were welcome. It stopped them in their tracks for the moment.

Mama lay on her day bed and she was magnificent. As the men entered the conservatory, she tried to raise her head to greet them but instead

148

gave a very slight consumptive cough and fell back on her pillows.

"What's the matter with her?" demanded one of the Danes, suddenly anxious he might catch something dreadful.

"It won't be long." Mama's "nurse" shook her head and wiped a tear from her eye. "I told her not to drink out of damp glasses."

You could tell Mama was really into her part at that point, or I think she would have hit Thomas for overacting. There was silence from the five men. This was not what they had expected, and they weren't sure what to do next. I was sure they were looking at Thomas suspiciously but didn't quite like to say what a strong-looking woman she was.

"Where are the Jews?" one of them demanded.

"Jews?" said Papa, looking confused. He stretched out his hands in a display of total honesty. "You may search where you like. We have been too busy with poor Marie."

"The greatest actress ever to grace the Danish stage." The "nurse" sniffed and began to weep silently.

I think the men were embarrassed. They glanced through to the other rooms and stared straight at the false wall. With the dim lighting and the potted plants, it was impossible to tell that it wasn't the end of the apartment. Suddenly, one of the men looked at Mama.

"I've seen you at the theater. How do we know you're not just acting sick? Come on, get up," and with that he pulled the covers off Mama with one rough move. Thomas gave a little shriek. Mama's legs lay exposed to all. They looked awful. The man was mortified.

"Oh God, sorry, I'm so sorry." Clumsily he tried to cover Mama up again, but Thomas gave him a little slap on the hand and he stumbled back out of the way. Things were going well. Mama gave a slight cough again and beckoned the SS officer to come closer. He leaned down toward her and she whispered with great intensity:

"... But that I am forbid
To tell the secrets of my prison house,
I could a tale unfold whose lightest word
Would harrow up thy soul, freeze thy young
    blood,
Make thy two eyes like stars start from their
    spheres,
Thy knotted and combined locks to part,
And each particular hair to stand on end,
Like quills upon the fretful porcupine."

The officer nodded. He had no idea what it meant or that it was from Shakespeare's *Hamlet*. He stood up and cleared his throat and looked sympathetically at Papa.

"She's not well, is she?"

Papa shook his head in sorrow.

"It's the drugs," sighed the "nurse," and took Mother's pulse for the tenth time. Even though I thought both Mama and Thomas had gone too far, I also thought it had worked and that the men were about to leave. That was when Uncle Johann gave a loud moan. It made everyone jump.

"What was that?" said the SS officer.

Everyone looked at everyone else. Uncle Johann moaned again. You could have cut the tension in the room just as Mama had done her legs.

"It's the cow," said Masha, who, to be fair, had spent more time in the yard than anyone else that summer and presumably knew the cow pretty well.

"A cow? In the middle of the city?" scoffed the men.

"Come and look," I said, jumping up. The men came to the window and looked down at Mrs. Jensen's cow.

"For the milk," one of the men, who had grown up in the country, said with a smile.

"Actually, the taxi driver runs his car on her poo," I said.

There was a pause. I think the men might have been thinking they had entered a mad house. The SS man looked down at the plants on the shelf below him. He was standing right in front of the geranium with the hidden gun in it. I had shoved the gun in rather hastily, and there was earth spilled all over the white woodwork.

"What's this?" said the man, and put his hand down to the plant. I think the entire flat held its breath. Had he seen the gun? At last he held up what had attracted his attention. It was one of my toy soldiers.

"Look," he declared, laughing, "I have found the whole of the Danish army." Everyone laughed. Uncle Johann moaned again and everyone laughed louder. Thomas took Mama's pulse. He was beginning to rub her wrist raw.

"Enough, enough," he declared. "Miss Skovlund must rest."

"Sorry, so sorry, of course." The five men bowed and the German clicked his heels.

"Miss Skovlund, it has been an honor. I have passed many happy hours in your company at the theater. My apologies for the inconvenience and best wishes for a speedy recovery."

With what seemed like her final effort, Mama presented the officer with her hand to kiss and then apparently fell back in a dead faint. The men hurried from the room to go and search somewhere else. Papa followed them to the front door, and they were nearly gone when one of them reached down to the newly positioned hall rug. Papa swallowed hard, fearing the man would move the rug and see Johann's blood, but he simply straightened the carpet, stood up, and said, "Could have a nasty accident with that if you're not careful."

"Yes, thank you," managed Papa.

And then the men were gone and the door was closed. Everyone was still too scared to celebrate, so we left the lights low and talked in excited whispers. Mama hit Thomas for overacting and he said he was appalled at the length of her Shakespeare quote. It was, without doubt, Mama's finest theatrical performance. I never forgot it because, sadly, it would also be her last.

So far things had gone well, but our friends could not stay behind the wall forever. It was not safe to stay hidden in the apartment. It was time to get moving. They had to get to Sweden and to freedom. The word on the street was that two German freighters, the *Donau* and the *Vaterland*, were on their way to Copenhagen to collect the Danish Jews and take them to the concentration camps. By now there were already several million dead in the Nazi gas chambers, although of course we still didn't know that for sure. All we had was rumor, but none of what we heard was good.

Papa called out the local doctor to see to Mama and Uncle Johann. Dr. Paulsen was an old man who had delivered all of us at home and he knew my father well.

"What is the plan?" asked Papa anxiously as soon as the doctor arrived with his large black medical bag.

The doctor shook his head. "There is no plan, Peter. No one expected this to happen. We are just having to make it up as we go along. Hundreds of families like you have Jewish friends staying with

154

them till we can get them across the water to Sweden. They say there are many people hiding in a warehouse on Asiatisk Place in Christianhaven. Come here, Johann, let me." The doctor looked at Uncle Johann's head and tutted. "That's quite a crack. I expect you saw stars for a bit."

He took out a needle and thread and began to stitch Johann's wound together. "I know for a fact that there is a large number of refugees at Bispebjerg Hospital," he continued. "Now everyone is working as hard as they can to get them transport to freedom, but it won't be easy."

"What do you think we should do?" asked Papa.

The doctor shrugged. "It is dangerous but I think you should take everyone to the hospital. My wife is a nurse there. She'll look after them."

Mama's legs were very painful. Maybe it was the makeup on the wounds or maybe she had become too thin worrying about Orlando, but her legs had become badly infected. She sat holding Thomas's hand. "I don't know what I shall do without you, Thomas," she sighed.

"Don't be silly, Marie, I can't possibly leave you."

Mama shook her head. "Thomas, my beloved friend, you must go. It isn't safe. Go to Sweden. All this madness will be over soon and then we can be together again. I need you to stay safe. I couldn't bear it if anything happened to you. Please. Go and change. Hurry."

I don't think Thomas would have gone if Mama hadn't pleaded with him. He kissed her forehead and went to change back into his suit. Mama was in agony and the doctor gave her morphine to help with the pain. Soon she drifted away from us.

Papa showed Dr. Paulsen to the door. He patted Papa on the arm.

"I will come for all of you this evening, Peter. Wait till then and don't go out."

The apartment was quiet after that as we all waited for night to make the next move. Anton and I played checkers while Papa paced and chewed on his pipe. Mr. and Mrs. Isak made sandwiches for everyone, but Uncle Johann wouldn't eat. He was more subdued than I had ever seen him. Spending time with the frightened Beilins and the feisty elderly couple had done him no end of good. Both he and Papa kept apologizing to each other.

"I didn't think it through," said Johann. "I believed what people said. I was just scared. I don't have a family like you, Peter. I didn't have anyone to talk to about it."

"I should never have believed you would betray us," said Papa.

"It was a good punch though, little brother," said Johann admiringly, rubbing his tender jaw.

Anton and I had always thought it would be fun to live in the same flat, but this wasn't how we had imagined it. We talked a bit about him going to Sweden. I was almost jealous.

"It'll be fun. No Gestapo and they have chocolate and chewing gum in Sweden," I enthused.

"I'll send you some," Anton declared, trying to look pleased about the sweets, but when it came to it, there was too much family trouble for anyone to relax.

Anton's dad was very unwell. He didn't want to come out from behind the false wall, and we weren't sure we could get him away from the apartment. He sat holding his wife's hand while Thomas looked after Gilda.

That evening a Falck—a kind of ambulance—pulled up outside the flats. It was a large black car with white wheel arches and bumpers and a cross on the front that our doctor friend had special permission to operate twenty-four hours a day. It was decided that the Beilins, Mr. and Mrs. Isak, and Thomas should all be transferred to Bispebjerg Hospital in the doctor's car. Uncle Johann would go along to help make arrangements for them, and after much pleading I was allowed to go to.

"They'll need someone to run messages and keep a lookout."

Papa was so preoccupied with Mama that I don't think he really knew what was going on. Masha had taken over running the house, and she made us sandwiches for the journey.

Uncle Johann gave instructions: "No one is to bring a suitcase—it would attract suspicion—so you need to wear as many clothes as possible."

Everyone took this very seriously. Anton wore two pairs of trousers, two sweaters, two coats, three pairs of socks, a hat, a scarf, mittens, and his sturdy boots. He looked like he was going to the Arctic. People thought of the oddest things they wanted to take with them. Mrs. Beilin wanted to bring a bag of socks that needed darning, and she was worried that she hadn't dusted properly before she left. Papa promised to look after everything, and Masha said she would darn the socks. This seemed unlikely but it was sweet of her to say it anyway.

We waited till nightfall, and I could hear Papa and Uncle having a heated discussion in the kitchen.

"I thought you said you had learned a lesson." I could hear Papa's voice rising in anger.

"Well, yes," replied Uncle Johann defensively, "I have—but he's not even a proper man. He dressed as a nurse, for God's sake. He might give us all away. How do you know you can depend on him?"

"I would trust my life to Thomas," said Papa quietly, and that was the end of the matter.

"Why doesn't Uncle Johann like Thomas?" I asked my father later while we checked the batteries in my flashlight.

"The world is afraid, Bamse, of anything that is different. It might be Jews or Gypsies or witches or anything that they don't really understand. You must stand up for everyone's right to be who they are—otherwise you may find one day that it is you who is singled out, who is seen as different, and then there will be no one to defend you."

After that I felt a great responsibility for everyone, so just before we left I went into the conservatory and dug up Orlando's gun again. I gave it a cleaning and stuck it in the waistband of my trousers under my sweater. It was probably foolish. I should have remembered Chekhov's words that Mama had quoted: that you couldn't have a gun without it going off at some time. I didn't really know how to handle the thing, and I was getting more and more frightened and yet I wanted to help. The Falck arrived and one by one our party slipped from the apartment into the back of the car. Thomas carried Gilda with her precious teddy bear, and Uncle Johann sat in the front beside the doctor.

"On the run in our own country," muttered Mr. Beilin. It was the first thing he had said for days.

"But at least we are saved by our own countrymen," said Mr. Isak, and patted him on the arm.

At the hospital everything seemed to be running smoothly. Our small group was admitted under the names of Jensen and Hansen. The doctors and nurses seemed oblivious to the brave act they were involved in.

"If we asked everyone why they thought they were sick, we'd never get anything done," sniffed one nurse, and she wrote down the name of yet another member of the "Hansen" family who needed "immediate treatment." After that our frightened little group was taken down into the basement, where we walked along a tiled white corridor that smelled of disinfectant and something else that I couldn't identify.

"Uncle Johann, what is that smell?"

"Formaldehyde," he muttered. We were heading for the mortuary—the place where the hospital kept those who had passed on. The living hiding among the dead. Others were on wards, in the boiler room, the chapel, anywhere the staff could find a space.

There was quite a crowd in the mortuary—every kind of person you might see on a Copenhagen street, from little girls like Gilda to ancient grandmothers, from strong young men who dressed just like Orlando to long-bearded Jews wearing peasant coats and skullcaps. There were men wearing suits and hats as if they were going to the office and women with new babies. All life was here. I recognized Adolph Meyer, the head of the children's hospital in Copenhagen. How could that be? A distinguished doctor, who had once saved Masha from pneumonia, hunted like an animal.

People were sitting on the floor, waiting. Waiting for something to happen, good or bad. More kept coming. The University Rifle Club had two hundred volunteers out combing the parks and other areas to see if anyone had been left behind. They found tired and weak people who had eaten almost nothing for days.

A doctor appeared with a clipboard. "Right, well, I'm sorry you have all been so unwell. The general consensus is that you all need to breathe some fresh air, so a boat trip to Sweden is being organized for your health. Now then, passage is going to cost two thousand kroner per person."

There was much murmuring at this large sum of money. It was enough to keep an average family for two years.

The doctor held up his hand. "Don't worry. No one will be left behind if they can't pay, but I would ask anyone who can contribute more to the common fund to do so for the sake of their fellow passengers. Now, as far as we know, there are currently 'health trips' leaving to Sweden from twenty-seven points along the coast of Zeeland from Udsholdt in the north to Hennaes in the south and we just need a little time to sort you all out with a passage."

The doctor began working out groups who would travel together. What had begun as a well-meaning but disorganized attempt to help was quickly becoming ordered. Uncle Johann and I were trying to calm people and help them. It was a mixed crowd. Unable to carry luggage, some people were wearing furs and several sweaters even though outside it was warm and dead calm: they were wearing their lives on their backs. One woman had so many rings on her fingers that she couldn't bend them. I saw an actor who had often worked with Mama at the theater. He was dressed like Humphrey Bogart. He had clearly decided to treat the whole thing as if he were playing a part in a spy film, and I knew Mama would have approved.

One woman, who must have been at least ninety years old, was very distressed. She grabbed my hand and began crying, "I don't have my dress for my funeral. I left it behind. What will happen if I die and I don't have my dress?"

Urban Hansen, who would later become Lord Mayor of Copenhagen, overheard her. "There isn't time," he said. "We are saving people, not clothing."

The doctors sent me out to see if I could find any more people still hiding. I borrowed a bicycle from a nurse and set out toward the docks. The streets were strange, deserted, and yet the heavy tread of German boots could be heard everywhere. It was like cycling through a bad dream. I was terrified but I was still my mother's son. I knew where the old woman lived and thought maybe I could pick up the funeral dress at the same time. I didn't see how it would hurt. I had learned from Mama that being properly dressed for every part was important in life.

ACT III, SCENE SIX
TIME: October 1943
PLACE: Copenhagen

I was scared to be out after curfew, so I kept to the side streets. I wished I had never taken the gun with me. I could feel the weight of its metal against my stomach and I didn't feel bold at all. I wanted to be at home with Mama or standing in the wings of the theater, knowing this was all a play and would soon be over. I thought about Anton hiding in the hospital cellar and wished he could have come with me. It wasn't fair that my daring friend was the one who was locked up.

I knew I had no choice but to be brave. Brave like the man who owned the bookshop across from the Nazi headquarters at Dagmarhus. In full view of the German high command, he was helping to organize transport to fishing boats and escorting people in their flight to Sweden. Each day the refugees would know that if there was a copy of poems by Kaj Munk in the window, then it was safe to come in.

I thought about Kaj Munk, the Danish playwright and priest, who had never stopped standing up and speaking out against the Nazis. Mama had appeared in one of his plays, *Ordet* —*The Word*—about whether miracles can exist. I couldn't remember what the play decided, but I knew we needed one now.

My route to the old lady's flat took me past Langelinie Pier. As I approached I could see the German freighters, the *Donau* and the *Vaterland*, standing by to take their human cargo on the four-day trip from Langelinie to Swinermunde in Germany and then cattle car to Theresienstadt concentration camp in Czechoslovakia. Word was that of the seven or eight thousand Jews in Denmark, the Germans had managed to capture only about two hundred and eighty. These were mainly old people or some who hadn't heard the news because they lived out in the country. It was an evil night. I stopped in the shadows to watch, leaning against the bicycle handlebars. The truth is I felt sick and didn't know if I had the strength to pedal on. Down at the pier I could see one small figure after another, hundreds of them, being pushed up the gangplank to the boat. The old people from the Krystalgade nursing home—some so old and infirm they had to be lifted aboard on mattresses by crane. The mattresses doubled up and squeezed the patients as the crane took hold, and I heard them scream out in pain. What harm could they possibly have done to the German people?

Those waiting on the quay were huddled together like animals in a storm. Well-fed Gestapo officers began pushing, shoving, and knocking down old people, making them stumble and fall. I saw an old woman who couldn't get out of the truck beaten with the butt of a gun so that she fell from the back of the vehicle onto the ground.

I wanted so desperately to help but I knew I should get out of there. I was just about to get back on my bike when with no warning a hand reached out and touched my shoulder. I nearly jumped out of my skin. I turned and faced a man I had seen in the newspapers. He was about fifty and was wearing a naval uniform. It was Corvettenkapitän Richard Canman, the German harbor commandant in Copenhagen. I moved my hand to my sweater to reach for my gun, when he put up his hand and said, *"Immer mit der Ruhe, ich tu dir schon nichts"*—Take it easy, I won't harm you. He smiled at me and ruffled my hair. "Go home," he said, and walked away.

I didn't know it then, but it was Canman who, during those critical days, ordered all his coastguard boats to be sent to the shipyard for repairs. He placed all his command in dry dock so that the Danish fishing boats could pass unharmed to Sweden. Canman did that and yet one Danish girl, in love with a German soldier, gave away the hiding place of eighty Jews in a church in Gilleleje. As I said, not all the Germans were bad and not all the Danes were good. It wasn't that simple.

I didn't find any more refugees but I did find the old woman's funeral dress and carried it back to the hospital. How odd to be thinking about saving your life and about preparing for your funeral at the same time. Maybe that was what everyone was doing.

I thought I had had enough excitement for one evening, but I was just entering the building when I saw the lights of a convoy of trucks sweeping up the road toward the hospital. Germans—hundreds of German soldiers. They clattered out of the trucks and there was a lot of shouting as they ran to take up positions around the building. They had seen me and it was too late to run, so I just carried on walking, holding the dress, until one of them shouted to me, "You there, boy, where do you think you're going?"

"I've . . . I've . . . brought a funeral dress," I managed.

The soldier shined his flashlight at me. "You're that boy from the actress." I realized he was one of the men who had come to the flat.

"Yes," I replied, clutching the dress in front of me.

The soldier shook his head. "A funeral dress. I'm not surprised. She looked terrible. Off you go then."

I realized he thought my mother was dead. I wanted to say that of course Mama was fine, but after my meeting with the naval commander and now this, my heart was beating so fast I felt I was in danger of keeling over. It was ridiculous. Here I was worrying about a little lie and there were people who might die.

Inside the hospital the doctors and staff were all gathered in groups trying to decide what to do. The entire building was now surrounded. It was unlikely that the soldiers would begin their search until morning, but there were now over two hundred Jews hiding throughout the building.

"I brought your funeral dress," I said gently to the old woman.

"That's it!" cried one of the doctors. "We need to have a funeral."

The next morning, just after breakfast, the doors from the hospital chapel opened to a scene of great grief. Someone had died in the night and now a funeral procession was winding its way to the cemetery. A hearse led the way, followed by black doctors' cars and a variety of other transports bedecked in black ribbon. It was a slow and somber affair. As it passed, the German soldiers bowed their heads in respect and thus failed to see inside the cortege, hidden in coffins, under blankets, lying flat in the trunk and anywhere else they could think of, two hundred Jews leaving the hospital on the next part of their journey to freedom.

Things were becoming very dangerous indeed. Three days before, on Monday, October 4, eight fishing boats full of refugees had been seized just north of Sletten near the town of Snekkersten. Twelve fishermen had been arrested and the refugees sent south to the camps. Everyone knew that nothing was guaranteed. Getting out of the hospital was merely the start of the journey.

Uncle Johann and I went with the large party from the hospital to help. Once we were safely away from the soldiers at Bispebjerg, the two hundred refugees were split into smaller groups. Our little clan was dropped on a corner in north Copenhagen. The doctor could take us no further in his official car without arousing suspicion. We were to wait: someone from the resistance would collect us.

"The king wishes you Godspeed," called the doctor as he drove off.

I wondered if the king knew what was happening. Did he know about all the little trips and how afraid everyone was? We stood in the shadows—Mr.

and Mrs. Beilin, Anton, little Gilda, Thomas, Mr. and Mrs. Isak, and the old woman with the funeral dress, who seemed to have adopted me. Uncle Johann was getting anxious.

"Where the hell is this car?" he kept saying as he paced up and down.

After a while I noticed a smell. A bad smell. It could only be one thing: Jørgen Johansen's taxi. Jørgen came puffing up the street in his evil-smelling car. On a trailer, attached to the back, stood Bess, Mrs. Jensen's cow.

"It's a bit farther than I normally go," he called cheerfully, "so I thought I would bring her along for extra fuel just in case."

It wasn't the escape to freedom I had imagined. I had pictured a spy film, with passwords and secret nods in the night rather than a drive through Copenhagen with an old lady sitting on my lap and a cow behind us. It's no wonder no one stopped us. We stood out so clearly that no one could possibly have been so foolish as to try and leave the city that way.

Uncle Johann was mortified. "Really! This is too much, too much," he kept muttering as we puttered and poohed our way north.

We were heading for Snekkersten, where the Strait of Øresund, the water between Denmark and Sweden, is at its narrowest. It lies on the coast just below Elsinore, where Shakespeare's Prince Hamlet lived. Down in the cellars of the castle, there is a huge statue of the Danish mythical hero Holger Danske. They say he sleeps there and that one day, when Denmark is in trouble, he will awake and defend us.

"Do you not think now would be a good time for Holger Danske?" I asked my uncle.

He shrugged. "We seem to be doing pretty well on our own."

I hoped he was right. We drove north for forty kilometers, stopping once on the way to persuade Mrs. Jensen's cow to give us a bit more fuel. It wasn't very glamorous: fleeing the Germans by sitting on a grass verge waiting for a heifer to relieve herself.

Thomas started singing show tunes to jolly everyone along. Then he got some leaves and pretended to make a hat for himself. Everyone smiled but it drove Uncle Johann mad.

"Stop it, you nancy. We're risking our lives here and you just think it's a game."

I was shocked. "Uncle Johann!"

Uncle walked away from the group to puff on his pipe. "Not bloody worth saving. Not even a proper man." I knew Uncle Johann had come a long way in his thinking, but Papa would definitely feel there was still work to be done.

Silently we got into the car and completed the journey to the inn at Snekkersten. Here the innkeeper, Henry Thomsen, was taking people in, organizing transport, and making sure everyone got something to eat. There was quite a crowd in the place, and many of the refugees were restless and extremely nervous. Some had became hysterical, some were old and confused, many were sick, throwing up in sheer terror. Nachum the tailor was beside himself.

"I can't find anything. My wife and my kids and now I've lost my pen. My pen—I've lost my pen. My wife would know where it was."

It was odd the things people chose to worry about instead of facing more important matters. It was as if by mislaying his pen, the tailor had reached the limit of what a man can lose.

"Let me look," I said. Finding pens and funeral dresses—it was odd work for a freedom fighter. I found the pen dropped outside in the lane. When I handed it to the tailor, he wrote down his name and address for me.

"Nachum the tailor. One day I shall make you such a suit. For your wedding, I shall make you a suit." He kissed me on both cheeks and carefully put his pen in his inside pocket as we waited for news of his missing family.

Uncle Johann had been getting instructions from the innkeeper and he came to pass them on to everyone.

"Right, listen up, please." Children were shushed as the frightened Danes gathered around. "Nothing is going to happen until well after dark, and I need your complete cooperation. This is not an easy operation and yesterday things very nearly went wrong. When you are told what to do, you must follow the instructions to the letter. Yesterday's group went down to the beach with clear instructions to wait for a signal of the letter *A* by flashlight and then answer *BD*. When the signal came it was not the letter *A*, but some bright spark decided perhaps the fisherman had forgotten how to do the letter *A* and so the *BD* reply was sent anyway. Instantly, a searchlight hit the beach and everyone had to run for cover. In the panic one man had cut the throats of his wife and two kids and then his own. He never knew that just an hour later the boat for Sweden arrived safely. Do not try and take things into your own hands. We will look after you and, God willing, this time tomorrow you will be safe in Sweden."

I thought how proud Papa would be of Johann. How well he had done to change his mind and now risk his life. The dark came slowly and everyone huddled together. No one could sleep, so Thomas got us to play a game where we imagined the best meal we could order. In a dank cellar we ate consommé, artichokes, smoked salmon, roast beef, roast goose, and pineapple, and drank fine wine sitting at a table crisp with pressed linen. Perhaps we slept for an hour or two. I lay on the floor between my uncle and the old woman. She held my hand but I awoke to find that it had slipped from my grasp and she had stopped breathing. She had died in the night. Thomas laid her out in her funeral dress and she looked at peace. I had never seen a dead person and hugged Thomas tightly.

"She is free now, Bamse," said Thomas. "She doesn't need to suffer anymore. It's OK."

At midnight the innkeeper brought everyone buttered sandwiches of dark bread and told us to split up into small groups. Uncle Johann and I kept our little crowd of charges together. I think he was warming to Thomas, having seen how kindly he had dealt with the dead woman, but he still gave him some funny looks. Gilda was too young for such thoughts. Aware how terrified her parents were, she clung to Thomas whenever she could.

The weather had turned nasty. There was heavy rain and a gusty wind as we groped our way forward in the dark. Our party was to head for the harbor and hide in a stone barn until the ship appeared. A soldier passed on a bicycle drinking beer, but we ducked behind a house and he never saw us. Otherwise the coast seemed clear. We were just crossing the road to get to the water's edge when we thought we heard the sound of a car.

"Hide!" commanded Uncle Johann.

Everyone scrambled to get across the road, and in the rush Gilda dropped her teddy bear. She screamed out for her toy and everyone tried to quiet her. Thomas picked her up but she wriggled free and ran back to the middle of the road just as a Gestapo car swept into view. For a moment Gilda was blinded by the headlights but the car stopped with the little girl alone in the full beam. She bent down and picked up her teddy and watched as the soldiers got out of the car.

"She'll give us away," whispered Uncle Johann. Mrs. Beilin had fainted and Anton was clinging onto his father, who seemed dazed, as if he'd had a blow to the head. One of the soldiers bent down to talk to Gilda and then looked around to see who might be near. I pulled the gun from my belt and aimed it at the soldier, but Thomas pushed my arm down hard on the ground.

"No."

The soldiers looked toward the noise. It was then that Thomas stood up. He stood up and walked with his head held high toward the car.

"It's just the two of us," we heard him say as he picked up Gilda and held her close. "There is no one else here but me and my Gilda." Gilda clung to his neck and Thomas didn't look back once when the soldiers opened the door for them to get in. It was a long time after the car left before we were able to move again.

Our little group was numb with shock. There was no heart left in any of us. The Beilins' grief was terrible to witness. Anton was sobbing and I did not know how to comfort him. We carried on because there was nothing else to do. I'd so wanted to be a brave man but I felt like a hopeless little boy. Down by the beach we found the stone barn and led our friends inside. Now someone needed to go down and signal to the fisherman who was coming. Uncle Johann wanted to go and look for the boat himself but he didn't look well. He still wore the bandages on his head from his fight with Papa, and I think the whole thing with Thomas and Gilda had shaken him badly.

"Let me go, Uncle," I pleaded. "I'm smaller than you. I can hide more easily. You stay and look after them here."

In the end he agreed—mainly, I think, because Mrs. Beilin was desperate for him not to leave. To be honest I was happier out in the wind and rain. The terrible emotions everyone was feeling were too much to bear.

Outside, the weather had turned even rougher. The wind whipped around the barn, and out to sea I could see great white peaks on the water. I had been told to wait on the beach until I saw the fishing boat arrive. Then I was to collect the others and run out onto the bathing pier, where a dinghy would be waiting to take everyone the last hundred meters to their rescue vessel.

I ducked down behind a sand dune and waited. My ears strained against the wind as I tried desperately to listen for the sound of the boat's engine. At last I thought I heard a slight throbbing sound and I looked up. There was someone on the pier. I felt paralyzed with fear. It was so dark I couldn't even make out whether it was a man or a woman, but he or she seemed to be fiddling with the rescue dinghy. I had to do something. Finally, angry and exhausted after everything that had happened, I stood up and pulled Orlando's gun from the waistband of my trousers. Shaking with fear, I approached the person on the pier. Maybe Mama had been right about Chekhov, and you couldn't carry a gun without having to fire it.

"Stop or I'll shoot!" I called, trying to make my voice sound as grown-up as possible. The person put up his or her hands and slowly turned toward me.

"Now, Bamse, why would you shoot your own brother?"

It was Orlando. I couldn't believe it. It was Orlando! We threw ourselves at each other, hugging and dancing around in that terrible weather. He looked just the same but older. He had a beard now and his hair was shaggy. He ruffled my own hair and said, "Maybe you had better give me the gun, baby brother." Then he grabbed my arm. "Listen!" We stopped still. In the distance we could just hear the soft chugging of the boat engine.

"The dinghy is no good," called Orlando over the wind. "It's full of holes and the boat will never get near the pier in this weather. We'll have to find something else. Come on."

We raced off up the beach and past the barn and headed toward the village. At last we saw a rowboat in someone's garden. It had been nicely painted and was now used for flowers. Without a moment's hesitation Orlando began throwing the earth and flowers out of the small boat. I wondered if we should have asked, but he was in a hurry, so I jumped in and starting scooping earth out too. At last it was empty and we managed to haul the boat upside down. We picked up one end each and proceeded up the road with it on our heads. It was a heavy old wooden thing and I was really struggling but nothing on earth would have made me tell my brother that. Neither one of us could see very well where we were going, which is why we bumped straight into the local policeman.

"Hello, boys. Where do you think you are going?"

Orlando looked at the man. "Are you a good Dane?" he asked.

Taken aback, the policeman replied, "Well, yes."

"Then help us carry this wretched boat."

Without a moment's pause the good Danish policeman picked up one end of the rowboat and off we went again.

We got everyone from the barn into the boat. Anton and I stood on the pier for a moment and looked at each other.

"Good luck, Anton," I said.

"Thank you, Bamse. I'll send you some chewing gum."

We hugged each other. I tried to persuade Orlando to go to Sweden with them. He had done so much for the resistance and would not get off lightly if the Gestapo caught him, but he shook his head.

"There is no rest until the last Jew leaves Denmark in safety. We must go back to Copenhagen and make sure no one is left behind."

Orlando and the policeman rowed our friends out to the waiting fishing boat: Mr. and Mrs. Beilin, my best friend Anton, and Mr. and Mrs. Isak, heading for Sweden. I could hear Mr. Isak chanting a quiet prayer from the Psalms. Uncle Johann was exhausted. He sank down on his knees on the pier and he too began to pray quietly. I had never seen such a big man look so humbled.

Out on the water, there were German patrol boats and bombs in the water to negotiate. No one was safe yet.

EPILOGUE

They did make it. My dear friends were safe but the trip wasn't straightforward. They were stopped by a German naval boat but when the officer came onboard and looked down into the hold where everyone was hiding, he simply called out to his comrades, "Not many fish in here," and then let them go. Among the Germans there was little stomach for the persecution of the Danish Jews.

At last they saw the lights of Sweden. Anton said that it was astonishing after the endless darkness Denmark had suffered for so long. It looked like the promised land. Almost everyone had been seasick, but when a Swedish patrol boat came out and the skipper called out a Swedish welcome—*Ni skall alla vara hjartlig velkomma i Sverige!*—they knew that they were safe.

The resistance carried on until at last, on May 4, 1945, the German high command surrendered to Field Marshal Bernard C. Montgomery. The BBC broadcast in Danish that Germany had capitulated, and we ran through the streets of Copenhagen to cheer the king at the palace. I ran with my father, holding his hand so that we wouldn't get separated. On the way we passed a young German soldier with a gun who was standing still, apparently in shock. My father stopped and patted him kindly on the back.

"Don't worry, son, now you can go home," he said.

On May 5, the British 13th Airborne Division came to Copenhagen by plane. It was a beautiful time of year. The beech tree leaves were just opening. People sang the national anthem, *"Der er et yndigt land"* ("There Is a Beautiful Country"), and throughout Denmark every household placed a candle on each windowsill as we banished the dark.

Sadly the story was not all light at the end. Mama had suffered terrible infections in her legs from her cuts. In those days no one knew that morphine, which the doctor had given her for the pain, was highly addictive. It wasn't long before she couldn't do without it, and she was never really the same again. It broke Papa's heart. He stopped painting and worked in an office so that he could be nearby and look after her. Masha married a Danish soldier back from the war, and Orlando was hailed as something of a hero. He went to the palace to meet the king. Gilda came home on one of the Red Cross buses sent to Theresienstadt by the Swedish Count Bernadotte. Her friend Thomas had passed away.

**The rescue of the Danish Jews** lasted ten days, from the eve of Rosh Hashanah to Yom Kippur—September 29 to October 9, 1943. It was a unique and spontaneous act of moral courage. The Danish government and citizens clearly understood the Talmudic excerpt that reads, "Whoever saves a single life saves the entire world."

Some 300 fishing boats took part in getting 7,220 Danish Jews and 680 non-Jews to Sweden.

In total 447 of Denmark's Jews were sent to concentration camps. About 120 of them died because of persecution; approximately 50 died in Theresienstadt or other camps; about 50 committed suicide or drowned on their way to Sweden. In total, despite Hitler's best efforts, less than 2 percent of Denmark's Jews died.

The innkeeper at Snekkersten Inn, Henry Thomsen, died on December 4, 1944, in the Neuengamme concentration camp.

Approximately 3,000 members of the Danish resistance were killed during the war.

Of the 530 Jews taken from Norway, only 30 came home. One and a half million children from across Europe were gassed in the camps.

In 1944 the entire Danish police force was arrested and replaced by the HIPOs—the Danish *Hilfspolizei*, or auxiliary police, who were Nazis and very aggressive. Many Danish policemen were sent to concentration camps in Dachau and Buchenwald, which everyone knew were two of the worst.

On January 4, 1944, the Danish playwright and outspoken critic of the Nazi occupation Kaj Munk was taken from his home by the Gestapo and shot on the road to Silkeborg. His Bible was found some twenty meters from his body, as if it had been taken away before he was killed.

On June 6, 1944, while Allied troops were landing on a Normandy beach, a dozen Danish resistance fighters blew up the Globus factory on the outskirts of Copenhagen. The factory had been producing parts for the V-2 rockets that were inflicting serious damage on London.

On June 22, 1944, the resistance struck against the Dansk Ridlesyndikat in Copenhagen's Frihavn, the only Danish factory making small arms, antitank guns, and artillery equipment. Thousands of Copenhageners watched the building burn down to an empty shell.

Within two days the Schalburg Corps responded by blowing up part of the Royal Danish Porcelain factory, setting fire to the concert hall, the dance pavilion, and the Glass Hall of Tivoli Gardens, which until then had been an oasis of peace and calm. The Nazi high command moved two armored tanks into the center of the Town Hall Square to show they meant business. The Danes responded with a general strike. They put up a FOR SALE sign on the tanks and began asking the soldiers where they could get raffle tickets to win them.

It should be said that many of the Germans stationed in Denmark did not obey their orders regarding the Jews. They did not search the coastal trains taking refugees to freedom. Those who did stop refugee traffic often did so in a vague and halfhearted manner. When the German chief of shipping in Århus, Friedrich Wilhelm Lübke, was told to prepare the ship *Monte Rosa* to transport Danish Jews, he made sure it had engine failure. One German captain claimed that his radio was broken and managed to keep interfering with the frequency of the German harbor police. The occupying German soldiers were either over fifty or very young. Perhaps the older ones remembered their failure in the first Great War and hadn't the heart for it all.

Sadly, those who were most fanatical about their anti-Semitic task were the Danish Nazis who served as support troops to the occupiers.

Most Danish Jews returned to find their property exactly as they had left it.

AUTHOR'S NOTE

Not long ago, when my mother moved house, we came across a small wooden frame. Inside it lay a blue armband with a red center, a white stripe, and a small metal insignia. It belonged to my grandmother and it was awarded for her work in the Danish resistance during the Second World War. It reminded me of the wonderful stories my father used to tell of that time: stories of the bravery of average citizens who refused to allow the occupying German army to simply have their own way. I started to tell my ten-year-old son some of the same tales, and it occurred to me that there might be other boys who would like to hear about such a daring adventure.

A great deal is known about the part played by Britain and France in the Second World War, but perhaps less is known about the story of the Danes. Although this tale of Bamse and Anton is fiction, it is based on fact. The only reason I had to make up parts of it is that, sadly, my father passed away some years ago and I couldn't ask him to fill in the details. But many bits of the story I know to be true.

My grandmother was an actress and my grandfather was a painter. In fact, I wrote the story with a wonderful oil painting of my grandmother done by him looking down at me from my study wall. It is true that she cut her legs and persuaded the SS to go away when there were Jews hiding in her apartment. It is true that the family worked in the resistance and carried notes and information across the city and sometimes to Sweden. They did what so many Danes did—they risked their lives for their fellow countrymen.

I once asked my father why the family had taken the chance, and he looked at me and said, "Because it was the right thing to do." It is a lesson that we would do well to remember.

BONUS MATERIALS . . .

SQUARE FISH

HITLER'S CANARY
by Sandi Toksvig

1. The book opens with a quote by Edmund Burke: "The one condition necessary for the triumph of evil is that good men do nothing." How is this an appropriate quote for the book? Who are some characters—Danish or German—who do something to combat evil?

2. Why do you think the Danes were so cautious at first to outwardly resist the German occupation? Do you think *den kolde skulder*, the "cold shoulder" treatment, was the best way for the Danes to react to the Germans under the circumstances?

3. Why do you think King Christian X would ride on his horse through town every day during the first part of the German occupation?

4. Near the beginning of the book, Bamse says, "Grown-ups were supposed to tell you everything was all right, not look scared themselves." What would you do if your parents and all the grown-ups you know were afraid of something?

5. Do you think Bamse's mother's theatrical reactions to everything going on were always appropriate? Why is it important to sometimes be able to make light of a serious situation? What were some instances when Bamse's mother's creativity helped a situation?

6. Orlando says, "You can't just call people Jews and then throw them out of the country.... They're as Danish as the rest of us." What does this say about how Danes viewed the Jews during World War Two? Why do you think Danes felt this way? How is this different from the way other countries felt about the Jews?

7. Why do you think some Jews were skeptical about the Germans coming to pick them up and send them to concentration camps, despite the evidence around them?

8. Do you think it was wrong for Masha to be seeing a German soldier?

9. When Masha finally introduces Boris, Bamse says, "He had a name. I don't know why, but suddenly he seemed more human." How could Bamse forget that Boris, and German soldiers in general, are also human? Why is it easy to forget during war that the enemy is human? Why is this dangerous?

10. Why does Uncle Johann support the Schalburg Corps and the Danish Nazis? Why do you think he comes around eventually to warn the Skovlund family that their house is being watched, and even helps them smuggle Jews to Sweden?

11. How did you react when Bamse's father punched Uncle Johann? Do you think he acted too soon, or were his actions justified based on what he knew at the time?

12. Thomas is "different," and it's because of this that Uncle Johann doesn't like him. What makes him different, and why doesn't it matter? Why do his actions say more about his character than his differences?

13. Sandi Toksvig reminds us that during the war, "not all the Germans were bad and not all the Danes were good." Why do you think she emphasizes this point? What instances in the book can you think of that illustrate this point?

14. What is "the courage of an ordinary Dane"? Can you list any examples of this in the story? Why are courageous acts by ordinary people important?

GO FISH

SANDI TOKSVIG

What did you want to be when you grew up?

I wanted to be a human rights lawyer. When I was a kid, I was very taken with a TV show about a lawyer named Perry Mason and with a book called *To Kill a Mockingbird*. I thought it would be wonderful to help people in trouble get justice.

When did you realize you wanted to be a writer?

I come from a whole family of writers. My dad wrote books, and so did his dad and his dad and various aunts and uncles. My brother and sister are both writers. Basically I went into the family business. I learned to read when I was four and started writing about then. I think it took me a while to realize I might do it for a living.

What's your most embarrassing childhood memory?

Anything to do with sports. I couldn't even do a somersault.

What's your favorite childhood memory?

My dad was a TV news reporter. When I was eleven, the whole family went with him when he reported on *Apollo 11*, the first manned mission to the moon. I was in mission control in Houston when Neil Armstrong, the first man on the moon, stepped out onto the lunar surface.

SQUARE FISH

As a young person, who did you look up to most?

Always my dad. He was a magical person, full of stories and a great passion for life. Very sadly, he died twenty-five years ago. I still miss him every day.

What was your favorite thing about school?

I loved learning so I was happy to be in class, but my favorite thing was being in plays and musicals. When I was at school in Mamaroneck, New York, I had a wonderful drama teacher named Regina Frey, and she was a great influence on me.

What were your hobbies as a kid? What are your hobbies now?

When I was a kid I loved to make things, and that's still true today. I sew and weave and knit.

Did you play sports as a kid?

Never. I hated sports. I am quite short and always felt too small for teams. I am also not very interested in competition, so if someone can run faster than me, I am just pleased for them.

What was your first job, and what was your "worst" job?

My first job was in the theater in the West End, which is London's version of Broadway. I worked as a followspot operator at the Palace Theatre. My job was to help light the actors. Last year I found out by chance that my great-grandfather, who was an inventor, was the person who put electric light in the Palace Theatre. What are the odds of that? My worst job was working as an assistant chef in an old people's home. I was not good at it. It was not fair to the old people.

What book is on your nightstand now?

I am reading *Westward Journeys: Memoirs of Jesse A. Applegate and Lavinia Honeyman Porter Who Traveled the Overland Trail* because I am writing a new kid's book about an Irish family who immigrates to the United States in 1847.

How did you celebrate publishing your first book?
I had dinner with my kids, who are my favorite people.

Where do you write your books?
I live by the sea and have an office in the garden with uninterrupted sea views. I sit there, and when I need a break I enjoy the waves and the wind, which change all the time.

What sparked your imagination for *Hitler's Canary*?
My father had told me many stories about his own experience in World War Two. I loved the heroism of a small country refusing to give up its own people. He was always very passionate that we should realize not everyone in a country at war is either bad or good. It is important that we each make our own decisions to be the best people possible.

Could you tell us about your father's experience?
My dad is really Bamse in the story. His parents saved Jewish families by hiding them in their apartment the way I describe in the story. They were not Jewish themselves, nor did they have any Jewish friends. They could have been killed for their actions. When I asked my dad why they did it, he just shrugged and said, "Because it was the right thing to do."

What kind of research did you do while writing *Hitler's Canary*?
I love historical research and probably do too much when I am writing a book set in the past. I read as much as I can to make sure the facts are correct.

What was the most interesting thing you learned while researching *Hitler's Canary*?
That Denmark was the only country in the world to save almost 99 percent of their Jewish population.

Did you have trouble deciding what to fictionalize and what to keep as fact?

My father had already passed away when I wrote the book, so I had to rely on my memory of his stories and on the historical research I did. The book is a marriage of the two, so I didn't really feel like I was choosing.

What would you like readers to remember about the rescue of the Danish Jews?

That the story isn't just about the Holocaust. That we all may find a moment in our lives when we have to stand up for others, and we need to find the courage or evil will triumph.

What challenges do you face in the writing process, and how do you overcome them?

It is easy to start a book; it's not so easy to finish one. Writing a book takes patience and many long hours. There are times, usually about halfway through, when going out with your friends instead seems like way more fun.

Which of your characters is most like you?

I don't think I am really any of the characters in this book. If I had to choose, I would like to be like Bamse's mother, who seems like good fun. But sadly, I am not that theatrical.

What makes you laugh out loud?
My kids.

What do you do on a rainy day?

Usually I am writing. I always have something I should be getting on with. Otherwise I weave or knit or read. I also love to cook. We have a large kitchen, and making dinner for the whole family (we can seat fourteen at the table) makes me very happy.

What's your idea of fun?
I love going to the theater, especially musicals—so probably dinner with friends and then a show would be perfect.

What is your favorite word?
Passion.

If you could live in any fictional world, what would it be?
I never really want to be anywhere except in the present. If I could make up a world, then it would be one where I can see my friends who live far away in other countries whenever I want to and without having to sit on a plane for hours.

What's your favorite song?
There is a Danish song we sing at Christmas called "Højt fra træets grønne top" (High from the tree's green top), which I love. We celebrate Christmas Eve, and our tree has real candles on it. We have dinner and then light the candles. Once the tree is lit, we all join hands and sing this song. I love that moment of the whole family being joined together.

Who is your favorite fictional character?
Harriet the Spy.

What was your favorite book when you were a kid? Do you have a favorite book now?
I loved *Bleak House* by Charles Dickens. The man was a genius writer, and it's probably still a favorite.

If you were stranded on a desert island, who would you want for company?
My kids.

If you could travel anywhere in the world, where would you go and what would you do?

I have traveled to many places in the world already. So far, my favorite place is the Arctic. I like to travel with a purpose. I recently drove across the U.S. to try to get some sense of how far the pioneers journeyed in the 1840s. The next big trip I would like to make is to Japan.

If you could travel in time, where would you go and what would you do?

I would like to go back to around 1600 in London and meet William Shakespeare for lunch. Then I would go to the theater and see one of his plays while he sat next to me.

What's your favorite TV show or movie?

I think *I Love Lucy* was a piece of genius. Lucille Ball, who starred in it, pretty much invented situation comedy, and she was brilliant. I do a lot of comedy in Britain, and I owe my start to watching that show when I was a kid.

What's the best advice you have ever received about writing?

Books don't write themselves.

What advice do you wish someone had given you when you were younger?

Don't focus on your mistakes. Use them to move forward.

Do you ever get writer's block? What do you do to get back on track?

I don't ever get writer's block. I think that's because I have three kids and bills to pay. I suspect fewer women get writer's block than men because they don't really have time.

What would you do if you ever stopped writing?
I can't imagine. Teach, maybe. I am chancellor at Portsmouth University in England and love spending time with the students. I would also love to go back to college.

If you were a superhero, what would your superpower be?
I'd be able to make anyone who hated another human being suddenly experience the life of their enemy from within. I'd be able to make anyone have a sense of being in someone else's skin, of walking in their shoes. Maybe people would fight less.

Do you have any strange or funny habits? Did you when you were a kid?
When I was a kid, I was never seen outside without a peaked captain's hat on. I think I was hiding from the world. My grown-up habits are dull. I put ginger powder in my coffee every morning. I spent a lot of time in a country called Sudan, and they make coffee like that. They call it "coffee with medicine," and I believe it keeps me healthy.

What do you consider to be your greatest accomplishment?
My kids.

What do you wish you could do better?
Write. I am learning, but I can always point to much better writers.

What would your readers be most surprised to learn about you?
I am quite good at boxing.